3 0063 00351 5642

W9-CCW-042

CLAN

Sigmund Brouwer

tundra

Tundra Books, an imprint of Penguin Random House Canada Young Readers,
a Penguin Random House Company

Library and Archives Canada Cataloguing in Publication

Title: Clan / Sigmund Brouwer.
Names: Brouwer, Sigmund, 1959- author.
Identifiers: Canadiana (print) 20190155639 | Canadiana (ebook) 20190155647 |
    ISBN 9781101918494 (hardcover) | ISBN 9781101918500 (EPUB)
Classification: LCC PS8553.R68467 C53 2020 | DDC jC813/.54—dc23

Published simultaneously in the United States of America by Tundra Books
of Northern New York, an imprint of Penguin Random House Canada
Young Readers, a Penguin Random House Company

Library of Congress Control Number: 2019950334

Edited by Samantha Swenson
Designed by Leah Springate
The text was set in Bembo Book.

Spearhead image from page 254 *Archæology and false antiquities,*
The Library of Congress/ Internet Archive Book Images

Printed and bound in Canada

www.penguinrandomhouse.ca

1 2 3 4 5   24 23 22 21 20

Penguin
Random House
TUNDRA BOOKS

To Dorese and Roger Harrison and to Sharla McKinnon: Thank you for all that you have done to welcome me into the Fort Frances community. Dorese and Roger, thanks always for making your home my home—and for sharing your amazing stories with amazing meals. Sharla, much gratitude for your passion and dedication to helping students become story ninjas and to the difference you make in their lives.

Foreword

When I finished the first draft of *Clan* and shared it with some friends, I was intrigued when one of them suggested that *Clan* was just as much science fiction as historical fiction.

Given that the story is set in a time when dire wolves and saber tooth cats and mammoths have been proven to be part of the landscape, my first impulse was to disagree. Along with extensive travel to museums—my favorite type of research—I had read a broad range of non-fiction titles to learn as much as possible about how Atlatl might have lived.

I had read the latest information and theories about Stone Age technology; DNA and language patterns of the First Peoples of the Americas; climate and geological changes; and early systems of justice.

With all of this background information, I had immersed myself in Atlatl's story, using what I'd learned to imagine life during the Ice Age era and placing Atlatl in a situation where he has to survive long enough to return to his Clan.

Clan takes place *before* recorded history, I told my friend. How could it possibly be considered science fiction?

The answer? Because there is no recorded history, there is nothing to tell us *exactly* how humans lived during Atlatl's time.

I realized, then, the wisdom of that answer. Without recorded history, many conclusions of experts in their fields are based on educated guesses and speculation—the same speculation I bring to Atlatl's story.

Leathers, woods and baskets of reeds are ravaged by time and weather. All that remains, at best, are scraps, leaving little to confirm exactly how early peoples lived. Stone tools are much more durable, but many found today are confused with rock that has shattered naturally. Precise dating of materials is so difficult to confirm that there is almost no consensus.

There is also not consensus on how and when the First Peoples made it south of the vast ice sheets that covered most of the northern continent.

Happily, we do have tiny clues and shreds of evidence that scientists and archaeologists have unearthed that give us fascinating glimpses of the past and help us make the best possible guesses.

So in one sense, yes, *Clan* is historical fiction. Yet, like science fiction, you will be entering a world where any author who takes you there will be building on what is known but adding a substantial degree of imagination and guesswork.

At the end of the novel, I hope you enjoy learning about the confirmed historical foundations behind Atlatl's journey and I hope that it might lead you to further research for yourself, perhaps by visiting my website for a list of the wonderful non-fiction titles about early human history in the Americas.

Sigmund Brouwer

Part One

THE GREAT FLOOD

Chapter One

Atlatl's first warning of the saber-tooth was a snarl that echoed down the stone walls on each side of him. Atlatl whirled toward the sound of the snarl and froze at the sight of the horrible beast.

Saber-tooth. It was the distance of the throw of a spear away. Atlatl did not have his spear. He'd set it against a tree, just down the hill.

At this distance, a spear would not have helped anyway. Since a childhood tumble down a cliff, Atlatl's left leg was permanently twisted at the knee, and he was unable to put weight on it to throw with any strength.

The saber-tooth snarled again and took another step.

Even if he was capable of running—which, because of his knee, he was not—Atlatl was trapped by rock walls. This beast, then, was in no hurry.

Saber-tooths were heavy and broad, low to the ground. Shoulders wide and chest broad. Haunches bulky with muscle. Saber-tooths did not chase with a burst of speed like a cheetah. Saber-tooths needed to pounce from ambush, then sink the spears of their front teeth into the necks of startled victims or into the soft bellies of larger prey like a mammoth or camel.

Its orange-brown fur rippled as it lifted and set down each of its massive paws.

"I'm not worth your effort," Atlatl told the saber-tooth. He'd needed to swallow a few times just to work moisture into his throat. "I'm skinny. My bones will get stuck in your throat and choke you."

It was either force himself to speak in a calm manner that hid his terror or shriek and limp away as fast as possible. He really wanted to shriek and try to run.

He knew, however, that movement would make the saber-tooth chase and pounce. Life both as hunters and hunted taught children the ways of survival early. Those who paid the price for inattention—if their bodies could be retrieved—were wrapped in animal skins and returned to the earth beneath the tears of the women of the Clan, who would sing wordless tunes of mourning until the sun left the sky, their faces painted red with ochre. Stories of the person would be told around the fires so that no one would forget them.

What Atlatl wanted to do most was listen to the tremble in his belly and flee, knowing that at any second those great claws could dig deep into the flesh of his shoulders and back. But he refused to allow himself to die with those marks. If his body was ever found, he did not want anyone in the Clan to know he'd been a coward. Especially Takhi, beautiful Takhi. He wanted Takhi to cry over his death, not be ashamed of him. After all, he was up in these hills hunting birds to bring her back his usual gift of bright feathers.

"Go away," Atlatl told the saber-tooth. "I'm a Healer. I can cast a spell on you. I will turn you into a mouse and squeeze you until your eyes pop out."

It was an idle threat. Atlatl was not the Clan's Healer. That honor belonged to Banti, Atlatl's uncle. Atlatl was just a boy, almost a man, with a twisted left leg.

"I saw a giant sloth," Atlatl said to the saber-tooth. "A little ways down the hill. Much bigger than me. You can take your time. It will still be there. You do know that sloths move slowly, yes?"

The beast ignored Atlatl's promise of a giant sloth and continued to creep forward. Too soon, it would be close enough for a ferocious leap with terrifying jaws opened wide.

Atlatl knew he'd been careless and doubted he'd survive to learn from his mistake.

➤

This was afternoon, late in the summer.

Atlatl was near the edge of a high rock wall that overlooked the rounded grasslands and scattered clumps of trees of the Valley of the Turtle. It was a vast valley; the low set of mountains on the western side, purpled by haze, were at least a day's walk away. Far, far upstream along the river that fed this valley was Ghost Mountain, where the Clan never traveled. Beyond Ghost Mountain was the land of the gods, where the Turtle god had been bound by the others to save the peoples from his anger: not a place for mere mortals to tread.

Atlatl had climbed this high into the hills because he'd wanted a private place to experiment with a new weapon for hunting birds.

The idea had occurred to him the day before. Atlatl had been prodding clumps of grass with a long stick, hoping to force mice to scamper where he could swat them. A small snake had twisted toward him, climbing the stick. By instinct, Atlatl gave a flick of his wrist to fling the snake away, sending the snake end over end through the air so far that, when it landed, the impact stunned it.

Snake meat was a delicacy, so Atlatl ran the snake down before it could move. He raised his foot to smash the snake's head with his heel, but it came to life again. So he scraped the end of his stick along the ground, catching the snake mid-body, and flung it harder than the first time, once again amazed at the distance he was able to throw it with the help of his stick. This time, the snake landed and did not move. He'd taken it back to camp to be skinned, but his mind had been on the power of the stick, not the delicious cooked snake.

What if, he wondered, he could find a way to fling a stone in the same way, far enough to hit a bird at a distance?

He was in the hills because he didn't want women or children watching and asking him questions in case his idea failed. While they welcomed all that he did to help the Clan and never seemed to notice his limp, Atlatl wished he had two strong legs to allow him to join the hunters when they left camp. If he could arm himself with a weapon better than a spear, his father would have no choice but to welcome him on the next expedition.

Perhaps too, that same weapon would help him hunt for birds with bright feathers, and he could bring those feathers back for Takhi.

Alone then, up in the hills, Atlatl had spent the first few hours using a specially flaked rock, called a burin, to cut and scrape a stout branch he'd broken from a tree.

The backside of the burin was a rounded half circle that fit perfectly into his palm. The upper end of it was a large notched piece that stuck out like a sharpened beak. By holding the burin snugly, he could push the beak along bone or antler or wood to carve with precision.

Eventually, Atlatl had reduced the branch to the length of his arm. At the end of it, he left a short forked branch. He sewed a small pouch of hide between the fork. This, too, took time. He learned sewing from his grandmother Wawetseka, but did not have her skills.

The results, he felt, had been well worth his time and efforts. The pouch formed a small cup between the ends of the fork, secure enough to hold a rock. By using the stick as an extension of his right arm, he was able to fling the rock with force despite his twisted knee.

Armed with the new weapon and a stone, Atlatl had gone looking for birds and other small prey. Before long, screeching from jays had drawn his attention. These distress signals were to warn other jays of a small predator. If he could get close enough, he'd be able to hunt the jays and maybe even the small predator.

His stealthy approach had taken him up and into the gorge that led to the edge of the valley wall, lined on both sides with broken ledges of sandstone. Bushes had found toeholds among those ledges, and they sprouted outward in tufts of various sizes. The jays hopped among them, squawking in fury at something among the leaves.

Atlatl had been unable to see what was making the leaves quiver with movement. He had crept closer and closer, ready to fling his stone.

Until he had heard the snarl of the saber-tooth.

Now, as it approached in a low slink, Atlatl realized he should not have allowed himself to get distracted by his own hunt. He should have been on the lookout for the danger that came in a land filled with predators like dire wolf and lion and cheetah and short-face bear and saber-tooth—animals that would also be drawn by the distress calls of the jays.

This realization did him little good, because it was too late. Far too late.

Chapter Two

The approaching saber-tooth was just as absorbed in its hunt of Atlatl as Atlatl had been absorbed in hunting the jays.

"Ooh-la-laa," Atlatl began to sing. Perhaps a strange sound would confuse the beast. Everyone in the Clan agreed that when Atlatl sang, it was indeed a strange sound. "Ooh-la-laa. Ooh-la-la-la-la-laaa."

The saber-tooth swung its head from side to side as it tested the breeze that wafted over Atlatl's shoulder toward the beast.

The distance between prey and hunter was closing.

"Let me warn you," Atlatl said. "I am armed with a stone thrower that will make you regret this."

The saber-tooth ignored his warning.

"You give me no choice." Atlatl flung the stone from his stick. It thumped against the saber-tooth's shoulder, but served only as a distraction, as if a large fly had buzzed into it.

That might have killed a jay, Atlatl thought with a trace of satisfaction. Then he told himself that this was not the time to take pride that his idea for a new weapon was a good one. Not against a saber-tooth or dire wolf or short-face bear or lion. He was going to die with the useless weapon in his hands.

Atlatl backed up a few steps, bumping into rock wall with the screeching jays and bush directly above him.

The saber-tooth advanced.

Atlatl had no choice but to take a stance and try to defend himself with the pointed fork at the end of his stick.

"This is your last chance," Atlatl said. "Stop now or die at my hands."

With his right hand, he placed the butt of the throwing stick against the rock face behind him, holding the fork upward. When the saber-tooth leaped, he'd shove the top of the stick downward to make it horizontal, and step aside at the last second while holding the stick in place against the rock, hoping the beast would impale itself on the makeshift spear. The odds weren't great, but it was worth a try.

Atlatl readied himself. He felt the thumping in his chest. Would this be his last day? Would his body be found so his grandmother Wawetseka and the rest of the Clan could wear red ochre in his honor and tell stories about him at the campfire to keep the memory of him alive?

He smelled sweet blossoms. Heard the buzz of bees. Felt the warmth of the sun on his arms and shoulders. He wondered why he had never appreciated how good it felt to be alive until this moment.

If this was going to be his final breath, he decided he would think of Takhi, and how she sang at the campfires and how the flames reflected in her eyes. Did it matter now that Powaw boasted to all the other hunters that he would be the one to claim Takhi? If Atlatl dreamed of Takhi in his dying moments, then maybe he could fool himself into believing she sang her songs for him.

Then, without warning, a saber-tooth cub scampered down the ledge, between Atlatl's legs and darted straight toward the saber-tooth.

It was then that Atlatl noticed the saber-tooth's swollen milk glands and realized this was a mother with a cub so small it still suckled.

He also realized that, all this time, the jays had been screeching at the cub. Behind the saber-tooth was a small cave in the hillside that Atlatl had not noticed—the saber-tooth's lair.

The cub tripped and tumbled and bawled for help, rolling into the massive paws of its mother.

The saber-tooth lowered her head and picked up the cub by the nape of its neck. She turned toward the lair. Atlatl felt his ribs begin to move again as he drew in air. The saber-tooth had no interest in him. For now.

But just as he took his breath of relief, two dire wolves appeared, upwind of the saber-tooth, stealthy shadows detaching themselves from a small stand of trees between the saber-tooth and her lair.

They, too, had been drawn by the distress calls of the jays.

The mother saber-tooth set the cub down between her front legs and snarled at the dire wolves.

Four more wolves crept out from the trees and formed a semicircle around Atlatl and the saber-tooth with her cub.

Chapter Three

Dire wolves. Dark fur. Yellow eyes. Jaws powerful enough to crush the bones of their victims. With the intelligence of pack animals accustomed to detaching young mammoths from herds.

That intelligence was evident now.

The saber-tooth was a far larger animal than any of the dire wolves alone; she was broader in the chest, higher in the shoulders. So not one wolf committed itself to a frontal attack. Instead, they pinched in from all angles, moving together with the same creeping pace.

The cub gave a high-pitched scream of rage, and the mother roared. The wolves crept closer, forcing saber-tooth and cub back to the ledge, so close that Atlatl smelled the musk of their fur.

One wolf darted in from the side, drawing the mother saber-tooth in that direction. As it did, another from the other side pounced on the cub, managing to grab a front leg to drag it away. The cub howled in rage and swiped the wolf across the snout with its other front paw, raking lines of blood. The wolf dropped the cub and retreated. The cub dragged itself back to the mother on three legs, finding safety between her large paws.

Now the mother backed into Atlatl's legs, pressing him against the rock wall behind him. He could see the hackles of her neck and even the dust rising from her fur. Had he wanted, he could have placed his hand on the giant cat's back.

A wolf made a quick dash. The big cat snapped her head in its direction. Another wolf pounced at the same time from the other side, and the saber-tooth slapped it with a giant paw. Blood gushed from the wolf's shoulder. It rolled backward at the blow and came up growling.

The wolves backed away slightly, and the mother used a paw to nudge the cub backward, almost to Atlatl's feet.

The cub was not his to protect, but Atlatl reacted without thinking and scooped the tiny cub upward with his right hand. He glanced over his shoulder and saw an outcrop of the ledge above him. He lifted the cub to the ledge, where it bared its teeth at the wolves below.

Strangely, pressed between the saber-tooth and the rock behind him, Atlatl felt safe. The big cat wouldn't turn on him while the wolves had her surrounded. And the wolves couldn't reach him while the big cat was a protective shield of teeth and claws. But this safety would only last as long as the saber-tooth was alive.

His instincts told him that now was the time to climb.

He glanced over his shoulder again. He took valuable time to measure footholds and the breaks in the rock wall where he could find places for his hands to pull his body upward. He was grateful the wall tilted slightly away from him, making the ascent easier.

Another glance at the wolves. Two were moving in from one side. Three from another.

Any hesitation now would cost Atlatl his life.

Atlatl whirled away from the fight. He left his throwing stick behind. He reached high with his right hand, pulled upward and found another place to grip with his left hand. He found cracks to wedge his feet into and, leaning into the rock face, pushed up with his good leg and grabbed another spot higher up with his right hand. He took two more upward steps, relying on the strength of his upper body to compensate for his weak leg.

His face reached the level of the cub.

Atlatl saw that the cub's leg mangled by the dire wolf was bleeding where the fur was torn. He looked up, and for a moment, their eyes locked. And then the cub slashed out with the undamaged front leg, and tiny claws ripped across Atlatl's nose.

This ingratitude was so outrageous, Atlatl should have flicked the cub off the ledge and sent it to certain death among the wolves. But instead, he grunted pain mixed with laughter at the cub's feistiness.

He felt blood run down his face as he lifted himself onto the ledge beside the cub.

It kept snarling and hissing. Atlatl knew he should just leave the cub to its fate. But the cub had saved Atlatl's life by returning to the mother from the bush. Despite the pain he felt from the slash across his nose, Atlatl also found the cub's useless bravery to be amusing.

"If you try that again, I will pull your entrails out through your hind end," Atlatl warned the cub.

The cub briefly stood on its two back legs and swiped a front paw at him.

"Enough from you," Atlatl said.

Atlatl waved his left hand as a distraction and again scooped the cub by the belly with his right. He lifted it above his head and set it on a higher ledge. Now it was truly out of reach of the dire wolves.

"Stay out of my way," Atlatl warned. "Or . . ."

He let a new threat die in his throat. The cub was doomed to die. The weak survived only if they had help. This was something Atlatl's cousin Powaw would whisper to Atlatl over the years. *You are weak. You are a burden. You only take from the Clan.* If their grandmother knew of this, she would be furious. The Clan always taught that kinship mattered most, that the Clan survived in a difficult landscape because everyone contributed according to their strengths, and that all had strengths. Atlatl wanted to take heart from his grandmother's compassion, but while his father Nootau never spoke of Powaw's taunts, Atlatl always sensed his father's disappointment that Atlatl would never be able to match Powaw's strength.

The cub retreated into a bush.

"So you *can* listen," Atlatl told the cub.

Atlatl pulled himself a little higher, until the cub was below his feet, peering out from the bush, still hissing and spitting at the wolves below.

The wolves had found their rhythm, darting in and out. None inflicted fatal wounds on the saber-tooth, but each slash of teeth drew more blood from the big cat's shoulders and ribs.

He could see the saber-tooth tire as it lost blood. Each counterattack came slower, and each snap of the head to protect itself was less certain. Atlatl winced. It could have been him down there, about to be torn apart.

He found a large rock and pulled it free. He flung it downward and it smashed into the head of one of the wolves as it moved in on the saber-tooth. Stunned, the wolf fell briefly. The big cat lunged, sinking the twin spears of its teeth into the wolf's belly. The wolf howled.

The saber-tooth pulled away.

Atlatl felt triumph for the big cat.

The feeling didn't last long. She was clearly tiring quickly. The battle continued until, as if by command, the other wolves sprang all at once and buried the saber-tooth beneath a flurry of savage bites and growls.

The end was inevitable for the saber-tooth, and Atlatl knew that once the wolves were finished with her, they might start looking for the prey that got away.

With the snarling and roars of the fight below him, Atlatl focused on saving himself. He was about to pull himself up a little farther when the cub leaned forward as if ready to join the battle below.

"Should I just throw you to the wolves?" Atlatl asked the cub. "Your death will be much easier than waiting among these rocks to starve once the wolves are gone."

The cub cocked its head and stared at Atlatl.

"No," he said to the cub. "You are not part of the Clan."

The cub moved closer.

"I'm telling you, you're on your own. You can't come with me."

As Atlatl watched, the cub nearly tipped off the ledge as his big clumsy paws scrambled for purchase. Without thinking, Atlatl reached out to steady it. This cub *had* saved his life, after all . . .

Because it was late summer, aside from the hide moccasins on his feet, Atlatl wore only leggings and a vest of scraped and cured animal skin, and his tool kit: a leather pouch with a long strap to hold it over his shoulders and against his back. Setting his tool kit aside, Atlatl pulled his vest up and over his head. He pulled the strap of his tool kit back onto his bare shoulders and wrapped the cub in his vest. It fought briefly while its head was exposed, but as soon as Atlatl wrapped the vest around the cub's head and blinded it, it grew still.

Now, at least, it couldn't slash at Atlatl.

With the vest under his arm, Atlatl climbed slowly and carefully. He didn't want to risk a misstep that would send him tumbling back down. Atlatl didn't turn until he was three-quarters the way up the ledge.

By then, the wolves were tearing into the mother saber-tooth where she lay motionless on the ground below.

Atlatl crawled the last short distance up and out of the gorge and began to limp down the hills to the safety of the tents and fires of the Clan.

Chapter Four

Atlatl held the bundle to his chest and awkwardly knelt at the broad and shallow river that cut through the Valley of the Turtle. The cub inside the bundle had not moved or made noise the entire hike back down to the water.

With his free hand, Atlatl scooped water onto his face. By how the cuts on his nose felt as the water washed away some blood, he guessed there would be no hiding the claw marks. When he returned to the camp, questions would be asked.

Atlatl straightened with his bundle under his arm and walked toward camp along the riverbank. Around the next bend, where the Clan's marker stone sat at the water's edge, the path would take him up the bank to where the women would be preparing food and the children would be playing.

When he reached that bend, Atlatl paused to examine the marker stone. Was it his imagination or had the water level changed?

The Healer was the Clan's spiritual leader. Whenever the Clan wintered in the Valley of the Turtle, it was tradition for the Healer—Powaw's father, Banti—to set an oddly shaped stone at the water's edge to give them warning should the water rise.

For when the world was formed, the other gods defeated Turtle, tied him to boulders and threw him into the depths of the bottomless lake behind Ghost Mountain. If Turtle ever broke his bonds, he would send the waters to flood the valley in retaliation. It was the Healer's duty to observe the marker stone each day.

Now, however, Banti was on an expedition with the men. So this duty fell to the oldest woman in camp, Atlatl's grandmother Wawetseka, the mother of Banti and Atlatl's father, Nootau. But she was too old to walk down the path to the river herself, and her vision was failing. She depended on Atlatl for help. It was his task, then, to go down to the rock every morning and every evening to let her know if the level of the shallow river had risen above the marker.

Atlatl frowned as he looked at the marker stone. Perhaps the river had risen. But if so, barely higher than the width of a baby's finger—so little, he could not be certain. There was no sense in upsetting Wawetseka unless he was sure. Atlatl memorized where the water level was on a notch in the rock and reminded himself to look carefully again in the morning.

For now, he had another concern: the tiny saber-tooth cub that was rolled in a vest under his arm.

➤

"Atlatl!"

He straightened and took a breath as he saw Takhi walk down the bank toward him. They were about the same age. Atlatl had noticed for months now that he always needed to take a deep breath when he saw her.

She reached the bottom of the bank and stepped onto the small flat stones that made up the shoreline at this portion of the river.

"You have returned," she said. If she were anyone else, he could have easily responded with any one of a number of funny remarks. After all, it was plain that Atlatl had returned. Otherwise, he would not be where he stood.

But this was Takhi. So he found it difficult to speak. Takhi wore bone decorations around her wrists and her neck, but Atlatl would have had difficulty describing any of them. Her voice. Her songs. Those were details etched in his mind. The softness of her glance, the curves of her mouth. Even the lines of her nose enthralled him.

Nose.

Not her nose. His nose. With claw marks still bleeding. He clapped his hand over it to hide the cuts.

"Yes," he said, his voice muffled. "I have returned."

She stopped a few steps from him and regarded him gravely. "You do not like my smell?"

As with many of her questions, it seemed like she'd tangled him in a net. To say yes would be an admission that he liked her smell. To say no, an insult. And a lie. He thought of how she'd phrased it. Or did yes mean that he didn't like her smell and no mean that he liked it?

Silence seemed prudent.

"Show me what you are hiding," she said when he took that prudent choice.

He grunted.

She closed the space between them and touched his arm.

The curve of her mouth. The lines of her nose. The soft glance of her eyes. And the touch of her hands.

All of those details he could describe. He remembered thinking of her songs as the saber-tooth approached and of hoping he could take those songs into the next life, believing she'd sung them for him.

She pulled his hand down from his nose.

"Saber-tooth," he explained as her eyes widened.

"Saber-tooth?"

"I sang to frighten it away."

"I'm surprised it did not fall over and die," Takhi said. "Your singing is a frightening weapon."

"Sadly," Atlatl said, "its death is one victory I cannot claim for myself."

She might like his story. He wondered if he should continue and tell her about the mother saber-tooth and the cub and the dire wolves.

"You were gone far too long," she said.

She'd noticed? His heart beat a little faster.

"The children missed you," she said, "and asked for you."

This felt like cold water on his face. Men were given the task of hunting; Atlatl's role was to herd the children safely while the men were gone.

"The hills can be dangerous if you are alone," she continued.

"Then it is good I have returned," he said.

"Of course," she said. As he tried to decide if that meant she might miss him if he were gone, she continued, "Without you, who will tell the children stories?"

This, too, felt like cold water on his face.

Then she smiled to show she was teasing him, and he felt like dancing.

Chapter Five

As Takhi left his side to join the women who were at the far edge of camp, Atlatl walked up the path from the river onto the upper bank. He saw the familiar tents made from cured animal skins, set around the fire pits in the center of the camp. Each tent was made with three camel hides sewn together, draped over frames and tied with leather strips. Rings of mammoth bones were set on the overlapping edges of the hides on the ground to keep the coverings in place.

Their Clan numbered twenty-five, one less than at the fall Gathering of Clans the year before. Twice each year—in the spring after the snows melted and in the fall before the snows fell—all the clans gathered in the same location to trade and celebrate. To show each other their tools and share new techniques of toolmaking. To tell stories about different places they had explored on the far-flung lands. To share knowledge about new finds of Precious Stone. Young men and young women from different clans would find ways to walk together. The young men would try to convince the young women to leave their own clans and start a life with them.

Takhi and her mother had joined the Clan at the last fall gathering. But three had been lost since. The first was Takhi's mother, who had been killed by a lion. The other two were babies who became sick and did not make it through winter.

At the edge of the camp, he saw the three young girls and the youngest boy of the Clan. The children were squatted around Powaw, who sat on the grass, dipping his hand into a basket of berries. Powaw must have been confident that none of the children would tell this to the women: the berries were supposed to be gathered and dried to save for winter months ahead.

Powaw had been born in the spring, and Atlatl in the fall. That difference in age would already have given Powaw an advantage in size and muscle even if Atlatl's leg hadn't been injured. After this winter, each of them would be old enough to join the men on hunts and expeditions. Because of his leg, Atlatl would be left behind at camp while Powaw would be given a chance to prove himself among the men.

As Atlatl drew near to Powaw and the children, Atlatl saw Apisi, the boy who was six summers old, reach for a berry. Powaw slapped away his hand, and Apisi yelped. The girls—Nuna, Kiwi and Wapun—gave the berries a wide berth.

Nuna looked up and saw Atlatl. He tried to keep his twisted leg straighter so that his limp was less obvious.

"Atlatl! Atlatl!" Nuna cried. She ran toward him, her face split with a smile. The other three children dashed behind her.

Powaw scowled. The children never ran to greet him as they did for Atlatl.

They skidded to a stop. Atlatl saw that their hands were stained with berry juice, but not their lips. Powaw was a stern taskmaster. He made them pick the berries but wouldn't let them eat.

Behind them, Powaw stood and made his way over. He imitated Atlatl's walk with an exaggerated limp, which Atlatl pretended not to notice. He did not want to give Powaw the satisfaction of knowing how much it hurt to be mocked by his cousin.

"Your face!" Nuna said, pointing at the slashes across Atlatl's nose.

"And what is in the bundle?" asked Apisi, pointing at the rolled-up vest that Atlatl held at his side.

Atlatl had expected these questions and had given them some thought. The Clan permitted some animals to live among them. Dogs, barely more than half-tamed dire wolves, traveled with the Clan. These animals followed the camp for the scraps thrown their way. They were valuable because they warned the Clan of predators, and their barking often kept the predators from approaching.

Atlatl could not recall, however, any stories about a member of the Clan choosing to bring an animal into camp for any other reason except to skin and eat it.

The cub, then, would be an exception of sorts. He had thought about trying to just sneak the cub in, but it would not remain a secret for long. His decision had been to act boldly, as if it was hardly worth remarking that he held the young of a feared predator rolled in his vest. If dogs could be part of the Clan, he would argue, why not a saber-tooth cub?

"My face?" he said to Nuna. "I was attacked by a saber-tooth."

She reared back in mock horror. "Like when you were attacked by a thunderbird? Tell us! Tell us!"

Joy at the prospect of another story from Atlatl filled Nuna's face. It had been many, many seasons since anyone in the Clan had looked up to see a thunderbird soaring against the sky—and some thought they were just made up by Elders of bygone days—but the children still loved hearing the stories.

"Not a thunderbird," Atlatl said. Powaw was now close enough to overhear his answer. "A saber-tooth this time. Large and fierce."

"You did not try to hide?" Nuna asked.

"These cuts are on my face." He grinned back at Nuna. "Not on my back."

"Atlatl would never run from a saber-tooth," Powaw said as he reached them.

This defense from Powaw surprised Atlatl. Powaw's father, Banti, and Atlatl's father, Nootau, were brothers, but as close to enemies as the Clan could permit within its small group. Powaw, then, considered Atlatl a natural foe.

"Thank you," Atlatl said to his cousin.

"He would never run from a saber-tooth," Powaw continued, speaking to the children, "because the truth is that Atlatl can't run. Everyone can clearly see that. He probably scratched his face when he fell into a thornbush."

Atlatl was suddenly very grateful for his impulse to take the cub with him. The younger ones were fully in awe of Atlatl, who delighted them with his stories, almost his own private clan within the Clan.

Too soon, they would reach an age of understanding. Next spring they would discover that Atlatl was not enough of a man to leave the camp for hunts. Then their adoration for Atlatl would cease. For now, they still hung on his every word.

"If I fell into a thornbush," Atlatl asked Powaw, "would I have been able to stand with a mother saber-tooth against dire wolves?"

"Dire wolves?" Powaw said. "Who would believe such a thing?"

"Dire wolves," Atlatl repeated. "The saber-tooth died and I escaped. If it didn't happen, how did I manage to take this, the cub that first saved my life when its mother had me trapped?"

Atlatl knelt, holding his bundle in front of him. He unwrapped the vest. The children gasped, impressed. The tiny saber-tooth blinked at the sudden light.

"You found it somewhere sick and dying," Powaw said. "The mother abandoned it."

Powaw reached down to poke the cub. With a snarl, it slashed at Powaw's fingers.

Powaw yelped. He shook his hand. Blood dripped from deep cuts.

"I will kill it!" he said as the children laughed.

"No, you won't," Atlatl said. "It saved my life. Now I protect it. If I find it hurt in any way—"

"There is nothing you can do to me," Powaw said. "We are of the age where if you strike me, I will take it to a Council of Elders."

Clan members fought together, not against each other. There were too few humans and the difficulty of surviving was far too great. If one Clan member hurt another, the Council of Elders would listen to each and make a judgement. The punishment could be as horrible as banishment. And humans did not survive alone.

"I would never hurt you," Atlatl said. He laughed. "But you might wake up with a snake under the skins that keep you warm at night."

Powaw recoiled as if Atlatl had actually held a snake out in front of him. Everyone in the Clan knew that Powaw was terrified of snakes, even small, harmless ones.

"Saber-tooths kill humans!" Powaw said. "It does not belong in the Clan. The women will listen to me. You'll see."

He ran back toward the camp as fast as if a snake were in pursuit.

The other children laughed and then gathered to watch the cub. It snarled again, but with less force.

When it snarled and pulled back its upper lip, they saw the half-grown nubs of the two large fangs that made it so distinctly a saber-tooth.

"Look at his leg," Nuna said. "He is hurt."

"And he needs food," Atlatl said. "We will find him a mother. Come with me."

Chapter Six

With the children following him, Atlatl headed to the far edge of the camp where the dogs usually gathered. Among them, Atlatl knew, was an old female nursing puppies. This old female was friendlier than most of the dogs. When Atlatl felt lonely, he would wander out from camp and tell stories to the dogs. Often, when he offered this old dog scraps, she would take them directly from his fingers without snapping at him.

The dogs were lying in a trampled area of tall grass. A few lifted their heads at the approach of the children. But they were familiar with the comings and goings of the Clan and showed little reaction. It was a hot afternoon and a good time to be lazy.

As for the old female, she was on her side, with the puppies nuzzling along her milk glands. They mewled as they sucked. At Atlatl's approach, the old female thumped her tail on the ground in greeting.

He sat in front of her, with the children behind and watching. One of the puppies staggered toward him, clumsy as it tried to walk.

Atlatl pulled the saber-tooth from his vest, careful to hold it in such a way that it could not scratch. He lifted the puppy and rolled it against the fur of the saber-tooth so that the little cub would have the same smell as the puppy. He did this again and again. The saber-tooth cub was becoming so weak it did not fight. The cub was not much bigger than the puppy, and the puppy seemed to enjoy the attention from Atlatl.

Now came the part where Atlatl needed to be careful of the old female.

Atlatl moved very slowly and set the saber-tooth among the puppies who were feeding at the old female's belly. The saber-tooth cub must have smelled milk, because, almost immediately, it latched on and began to suck. It closed its eyes in pleasure.

Atlatl backed away and sat in a circle with the children.

Moments later, the old female turned her head toward her belly. She sniffed at the saber-tooth. Then she licked

it carefully, cleaning up the blood from the wound on
the saber-tooth's front leg. All the while, the saber-
tooth rumbled in contentment.

"See," Atlatl said in triumph to his adoring friends.
"We found it a mother."

From a ways behind him came Takhi's voice again,
and as always, it made him weak in a strange way.

"Atlatl," she said softly. "Your grandmother calls for
you. Powaw has tried to convince her that the cuts on
his hand come from a saber-tooth cub and that you are
protecting the cub."

She laughed, a sound like that of cheerful birds. "And
I thought you were the storyteller, not Powaw!"

"Look, Takhi," Nuna said. She pointed down at the
cub. "It's true. There it is. Among the puppies!"

Takhi clapped her hands in delight. "Oh, Atlatl,
there is no one quite like you, is there."

Grateful as he was that the saber-tooth cub amused
her, he wished he'd been able to bring back his gift of
bright feathers for Takhi instead.

Takhi's laughter changed to concern. "But now you
will have to answer Powaw's accusations. Wawetseka is
waiting for you with the other women."

➡

Game was plentiful in this valley the Clan had chosen for their winter home. The hills gave shelter from storms. While shallow, the river was fast flowing and would not freeze when the snows arrived. Because the Clan made this a longtime camp, the ground inside the tents had animal skins as rugs. Among the campfires were chairs made from sticks bound to form a tripod, with a skin stretched across and sewn in place. When the Clan moved camp again, the chairs would be taken apart and the skins packed for travel.

Wawetseka sat in one of the chairs, centered among the women. Behind her, smirking, stood Powaw.

When the chatter of the women grew silent at Atlatl's approach, Wawetseka turned her head in Atlatl's direction. Her face was puckered. Her hands were shriveled. Her eyes were clouded. The only things strong about her were her mind and her voice.

Atlatl limped until he was directly in front of her. He often helped Wawetseka gather the plants they needed for medicine, and they spent those hours chatting like old friends. In front of the women, however, he acknowledged her revered position in the Clan and respectfully waited for her to speak.

At this silence, Atlatl saw his grandmother flare her nostrils. Though she had lost much of her vision, her senses of hearing and smell were still sharp.

It would be an insult to tell her he had arrived. She would know he was there. And she did.

"So," she said. "One of my grandsons makes an accusation against the other."

Atlatl needed no explanation for the sadness he heard in her voice. He understood how badly she wished that her sons—Powaw's father, Banti, and Atlatl's father, Nootau—would behave as brothers, not as bitter competitors. Each believed their strengths—Banti as Healer and Nootau as leader of the hunts—entitled them to be the true head of the Clan. Banti made no secret of his bitterness that Nootau was considered leader.

"If Powaw told you I brought a saber-tooth into the camp," Atlatl said. "It is not an accusation. It is truth."

Atlatl saw no point in denying something that could easily be verified.

"A saber-tooth," Wawetseka said. "And you set it upon Powaw to attack him?"

The other women remained silent as they, too, showed respect for Wawetseka's age and her knowledge. One was punching a bone needle through skin and drawing a leather thread to tighten two pieces of hide together. Another wove strands of grass into rope.

Atlatl could sense, however, that they were interested in the conversation.

"Yes, I set it upon him," Atlatl said. "It was a horrible attack. A huge beast. At least as large as this."

Atlatl cupped his hands as if he were trying to hold water to show how small the cub was. "When Powaw poked it, it leaped forth, almost knocking him to the ground. I pulled it from Powaw to save Powaw's life, and look what the ferocious beast did to me."

Atlatl pointed at his nose.

Some of the women giggled.

"Powaw," Wawetseka said, "move from behind me and stand in front of me so that you are facing me."

Powaw shuffled around from behind her.

"Did you poke at the cub?" she asked him.

"I didn't know if it was alive or dead," Powaw said, sullen, head down. "Atlatl should have killed it before bringing it into camp."

"I did not ask if it was dead or alive. I asked if you poked at it."

"Yes," he finally said.

"It did not attack you as you claimed, but defended itself?"

Powaw remained silent.

"To survive, the clan must always be united, and telling lies destroys our harmony. Furthermore, it is a grave offense to bear false witness to any Elders of the Council," Wawetseka told Powaw. "Even with a lie that seems harmless."

Powaw sputtered. "Atlatl just declared that it was a huge beast and that it knocked me to the ground! Talk to him about truth telling!"

"You are smarter than that. Or do you want to pretend you are not capable of understanding a joke?"

Powaw drew a deep breath, showing he knew any answer to that would make him look bad.

Wawetseka said, "I repeat, it is a grave offense to bear false witness to the Elders of the Council."

"I am not in front of the Elders of the Council," Powaw said.

"Yet you came running and asked me to make judgement on your cousin as if I were."

Powaw had no answer to that either.

Wawetseka sighed and turned her attention to Atlatl. "A saber-tooth, no matter how small, does not fit within the Clan. Saber-tooths hunt humans. Why should we set aside precious food to help it grow?"

Atlatl had anticipated this question and knew the

cub's life depended on convincing Wawetseka to let it stay.

Atlatl told Wawetseka about being trapped by the mother saber-tooth and how the cub had saved his life and how the dire wolves had appeared and how the cub was nursing from the old female dog.

It was a good story, and Atlatl knew it. He just hoped it was a good enough story to sway Wawetseka.

"You see," Atlatl said as he finished, "the cub saved my life. The Clan is strong because the Clan fights together to survive. The cub saved one of us, and it deserves to be one of us."

"I do not like this," Wawetseka said. "Nothing but trouble can come from a predator that grows large among us."

"See!" Powaw said. "See! Let me be the one to kill it."

Atlatl saw irritation across Wawetseka's face, and the women whispered among themselves. It was not Powaw's place to make this judgement. And he had interrupted her. Now if Wawetseka judged that the cub should be killed, it would look like she was obeying a rude boy.

"The cub will live among the dogs of the Clan," Wawetseka told Atlatl.

She turned to Powaw. "And if I hear of you harming it, there will be punishment."

Now Wawetseka turned back to Atlatl. "When the cub needs more than milk, the only food you give it will be minnows and small birds. Do you understand? Nothing of value to us."

This was a victory. It could have been argued that the time Atlatl spent in pursuit of minnows and small birds should be used to gather berries and roots to store for winter.

Atlatl nodded.

"It should not be long until it is large enough to fend for itself," she said. "When it is ready, you will take it into the hills and set it free. In that way, you will have repaid your debt to it."

"I understand," Atlatl said. This was as much as he could have hoped for.

"Now," Wawetseka said to Atlatl. "Tell me about the marker stone. Has the water at the river risen at all?"

"No," Atlatl said without flinching. Why should he upset his grandmother over something as small as a change in the river that might only be his imagination?

Chapter Seven

Atlatl sat atop the grassy flatlands above the river, in shouting distance of the women. Cub was stretched out on the ground beside Atlatl, snoring. Since surviving the attack of the dire wolves, the cycle of the moon had passed from full to dark to full again, and the men would be returning any day.

The children were laughing and playing behind him, and their joyfulness added to his sense of melancholy. These moments hit him occasionally. Surrounded by the Clan, he still felt so apart.

He reached over and scratched the top of Cub's head, taking comfort from the animal's companionship.

On the first morning, when Atlatl had lifted Cub away from the puppies, Cub had given a token growl and halfhearted swipe, and then allowed Atlatl to carry him down to the river to check the marker stone.

On the second morning, no growl and no swipe. On the third morning, Cub had smelled Atlatl and leaped into his hands, something that gave Atlatl delight. On the fourth morning, Cub had followed him down to the river. That evening, Cub had found Atlatl where he was sleeping and had curled up against his ribs for the entire night. After that, Cub was constantly at Atlatl's side, only returning to the mother dog to drink milk.

In that time, Cub had grown twice as quickly as the puppies that he rolled with and playfully fought. The slash on Cub's front leg had healed, and these fights were rapidly becoming unfair in Cub's favor. As Wawetseka had predicted, Cub grew much larger and much faster than the littermates who had adopted him as a brother.

In one way, this gave Atlatl joy. Cub was healthy and strong. In another way, it caused only dread. Soon, Cub would be big enough that Atlatl would have no choice but to release Cub back into the hills to fend for himself.

He knew it would be like mourning the death of a friend.

Atlatl closed his eyes and sang softly, as if that day had already arrived. This was how the Clan honored memories of the dead.

He felt a hand on his shoulder, and it startled him.

"I was coming over to ask if you would tell the children a story," Takhi said. "I could not help but hear as you sang."

Atlatl smiled to see the bright bird feathers woven into her hair. "And you didn't run away? Even though you believe my singing is a frightening weapon?"

"Your voice is not made to carry any melody," she said. "But when what you sing comes from the heart, that's what matters."

She sat cross-legged beside him. Staring at the horizon, she said, "Do you remember your mother?"

He knew why she was asking. She had lost her mother too.

"No," he said. "I wish I did. I was too young when she died to remember her."

"Yet sometimes I envy you," she said. "Every day, I grieve for my mother. I remember so many things. Each night, I sing of her memories to myself. I can't remember my father, so I have no songs to sing of him. I have no tears for him. Nothing is there to hurt my heart. But my mother . . ."

Atlatl glanced at her. "I wish I could meet my mother and have memories of her to mourn, so I guess it's hard no matter what." He plucked a blade of grass and studied it. "People say I take after her. She liked to tell stories too. I certainly don't take after my father. He—"

He stopped himself. His burden should not be hers.

"Yes?" she asked.

Atlatl stood, trying not to show the weakness of his twisted knee. He flashed her a grin, as if they had merely been discussing whether it might rain.

"The children," he said. "You wanted me to tell them a story?"

He tried to minimize his limp as they walked. Cub stayed with him every step of the way.

➤

With the solemn eyes of the Clan's children upon him, Atlatl set down a large dark rock on the edge of the upper bank and pretended to study its placement on the grass. After a few seconds of consideration, he nodded with satisfaction. Much of good storytelling was good acting.

"Now," he asked his audience, "are you sure you shouldn't be looking for grubs?"

"Thunderbird! Thunderbird!" This response came from little Nuna, and the other young ones echoed her enthusiasm. Powaw simply shrugged, either not caring or wanting it to appear he didn't care. Atlatl often wondered why Powaw stayed nearby, when he tried to make it so obvious that nothing Atlatl did interested him.

"Not the bison dung story?" Atlatl said, grinning at Powaw. A few years earlier, Atlatl had dug a hole along a path between trees. He had filled it with fresh bison dung and covered the dung with leaves. He had then strung a grass-braided rope at knee height between the trees. He'd provoked Powaw into chasing him down the path. It looked like an unfair contest, with Powaw rapidly gaining on Atlatl and mocking Atlatl for his slow limp. With a one-legged hop, Atlatl had jumped over the rope and then another hop took him sideways to avoid the bison dung. Powaw, however, had tripped on the rope and fallen face-first into the dung. Better yet, Powaw had bellowed with rage as he stumbled around with dung clinging to his body, drawing in most of the Clan, who all laughed uproariously at Atlatl's prank.

"First the thunderbird story," Nuna said. She was the youngest, born five summers earlier.

"Then the thunderbird story it will be," Atlatl said. Taking a rock of similar size and color to the first, Atlatl took two measured paces, then stopped, squinting with seriousness as he surveyed the ground.

On the upper bank of the river, there was enough breeze to blow away irritating insects, and already it was warm.

Atlatl spoke in a dramatic hush. "It is a bird so large that when it flaps to leave the ground, it makes thunder with its wings and draws thunder from the skies. Its wingspan is the distance between these rocks."

"We already know about the noise," Powaw said. He turned to the other children. "It's why the Elders call them thunderbirds. And because when it appears, storms with thunder often follow."

Perhaps, Atlatl thought, Powaw made a habit of following him just for any chance to show scorn.

"No, Powaw!" Nuna said. "Let him tell his story!"

Powaw crossed his arms and tightened his lips.

Atlatl took satisfaction that the power of story still gave him a degree of control over Powaw.

"I was a small child," Atlatl said. "I was playing at the edge of a bank, much like this one. I remember looking over the edge. A large shadow covered me. It knocked me over the edge and then I fell. A large bush held me from falling too far; otherwise, I would have tumbled down to the river and drowned."

Atlatl closed his eyes briefly. Although he told the story often, the only things truly clear in his mind were a brief glimpse of the large shadow, the sensation of falling, the shattering pain of his broken knee against a boulder and his clinging to a bush and crying for help. The first of the Clan to arrive had been Powaw's father, Banti, who had peered over the cliff and then gone to get help. Since Atlatl didn't exactly remember the thunderbird itself, many details of his story came from his grandmother: in her childhood, she said, there were thunderbirds large enough to carry away babies, and she had told him many times about seeing them.

Yet it was with the confidence of a storyteller that Atlatl continued. "I was not going to let a thunderbird carry me to its nest and tear me apart to feed its young. To protect myself, I grabbed a sharp-edged rock and stood ready to defend myself."

"Your leg," Apisi said. His face was smudged with dirt. He spoke with a lisp through a huge gap in his front teeth. "We all know that the fall broke your leg. How could you stand if your leg was broken?"

That was true. The fall had shattered Atlatl's leg, leaving him with his permanently twisted knee.

In all his tellings of this heroic story about the day he battled a thunderbird, not once had any of the children asked him this question. It gave Atlatl pause.

Apisi glanced over at Powaw, and then back at Atlatl, his face set in defiance. There it was, Atlatl realized. The first sign of disloyalty. Atlatl often suspected that Powaw spoke badly of Atlatl to the children behind his back.

"My leg hurt badly," Atlatl said. "I was able to cling to a nearby bush and pull myself up with one hand. With the rock in my other hand, as the bird dived to take me away, I struck it in the head and—"

"Proved that, like every child in this Clan," Takhi said, "you are brave and wonderful."

Powaw said, "We all know that Atlatl makes up stories and begins to believe them. We just listen because it makes him feel better about himself."

"Without stories," Takhi said, "we have no memories. Without memories, we are nothing."

"Memories should be true!" Powaw snapped.

"Memories teach us what matters," Takhi replied.

"I cannot believe you defend someone who . . . who . . ." It was almost as if Powaw wanted to speak aloud the taunts he whispered to Atlatl. But then he would face Wawetseka's wrath. "Someone who will never be able to bring you a deer to cook over a fire."

"In the Clan," Takhi answered, "we all have different roles."

"Atlatl is a great hunter," Powaw said. "After all, wasn't he able to kill something so large and dangerous as a bird with those pretty feathers you have in your hair?"

"Powaw," Atlatl said, "is that a snake near your feet?"

Powaw screeched and jumped. The children giggled.

"I have had enough of you," Powaw told Atlatl. "Enough."

Powaw took a step toward Atlatl.

Suddenly, a sign of loyalty to Atlatl came from an unexpected source.

Cub snarled.

Atlatl had forgotten about the saber-tooth. But the raised voices must have woken him. Now Cub stood between Powaw and Atlatl, front legs braced, and snarled again.

For a moment, Powaw recoiled. Cub was twice the size of the puppies now. Still not big enough to be a threat. But the snarl was impressive.

Then Powaw moved forward again, his face even angrier.

Atlatl shifted his weight, prepared to defend himself. He should have been afraid, but secretly he welcomed a chance to hit Powaw.

Takhi quickly moved between them.

"The Clan does not fight within the Clan," Takhi said. "You both know that. And you are old enough that if you do fight, you will face the Council of Elders."

"He mocks me all the time," Powaw said. "As if somehow he is better. Yet look at him. His leg. He—"

"Takhi," Atlatl said. "Stand aside. This is not your fight."

"I am trying to protect both of you," Takhi said angrily.

"Stand aside." Atlatl heard his voice rising as he fought his anger and frustration at the weak leg that brought him so much shame. He would lose this fight, but that didn't seem to matter. The important thing was that he *would* fight.

She opened her mouth to protest again, but it was Apisi who spoke.

"Powaw!" Apisi said, pointing back at camp. "The men! They have returned!"

Chapter Eight

*P*link. *Plink. Plink. Plink.*

Morning had come with blue skies and warmth. The men of the Clan sat in a circle to work on their tools and enjoy conversation. Atlatl was at the fringe of the group, holding his stone thrower, and waiting for a chance to talk to his father, Nootau, who had been too busy since his return to give Atlatl any attention.

Plink. Plink. Plink. Plink.

Atlatl was very familiar with this sound. It came from one of the hunters beyond Nootau. This hunter was making rapid, small strokes with the butt of an antler against a stone, sending precise flakes onto the ground in front of him as he finished his spear point.

Nootau and Banti had said little about the presence of a saber-tooth cub in the Clan. They'd accepted Wawetseka's ruling that when it was old enough to fend for itself, Atlatl would bring it into the hills and set it free.

Within the Clan, there were clearly defined roles, all of them needed for the Clan to survive. Some were specialty skills, like Wawetseka's. She knew plants—which ones were poison, which ones could be eaten, which ones needed to be cooked first, which ones were good for pains of the joints, like the bark of mountain alders, or for headaches, like the bark of willow.

The women taught the girls to braid grasses and leather strips into ropes, to weave baskets and sew clothes from animal hides using small blades to cut skins and sewing needles carved from mammoth ivory.

The men focused on toolmaking. Their pouches carried one or two preforms—stones already worked down to carrying size that could be then made into tools, like scrapers or blades or burin. A preform could also be fashioned into bifaces, the stone points that were knapped on both sides to form razor-edge spear points.

Atlatl wished his role in the Clan would be to lead in hunting, like his father did. But because of his leg, the men did not include him when they discussed plans of taking down large animals. The women didn't include him in their traditional work either, but Atlatl had learned from observation how to weave baskets and sew clothing.

Because he spent so much time around his grandmother Wawetseka, Atlatl was gaining knowledge about plants, but he still had a lot to learn. She liked to joke that she had taught Atlatl everything that *he* knew about plants but had yet to teach him even half of what *she* knew.

Now, inside the circle, Nootau was squatting beside Powaw. Nootau was a short and powerful man, much like a saber-tooth. He was broad in the chest, with a bowlegged walk and massive arms. Atlatl did not have any promise of his father's bulk. He was more slender, like his mother had been.

Atlatl wished his father was squatting beside him instead of Powaw. Atlatl craved a sense of belonging and acceptance among the hunters. For that reason, like now, he'd observe their techniques from the edge of the circle. They grudgingly gave him scrap stones, and he'd find a way to practice those techniques in solitude. It's why he had a grasp of toolmaking, even though there was little likelihood he'd ever have the opportunity to use those tools on hunts.

Plink. Plink. Plink. Plink.

The men were in good spirits. They had returned with enough big pieces of chert to sustain them through to the next summer. What they didn't use here, they would leave behind in a cache, saving them the long trip to the original source.

Chert was gray granite that was hard and durable. The men used chert for pounding tools or to work the more fragile Precious Stone.

As for the jet-black Precious Stone—which needed to be transported from hills far, far away—it did not hold an edge and needed constant sharpening. But it was easy to sharpen and capable of slicing through the toughest of hides.

Plink, plink, plink, plink.

"It is much nicer working stone when the weather is warm like this," Nootau told Powaw. "The stone responds as if it is alive. And your fingers are a lot more nimble."

Nootau had a huge block of chert in front of him. With a hammerstone larger than his fist, he pounded it hard with four or five blows. The block split into three smaller pieces.

Nootau handed a block of chert to Powaw, along with the hammerstone.

"Strike at an angle like this," Nootau said, showing Powaw the motions. As he spoke, claws on a necklace rattled on his chest. It was a mixture of lion claws and cheetah claws. Nootau had killed so many animals by himself that he had several of these necklaces.

Powaw made a clumsy attempt, with no results. Frustrated, he glanced at Atlatl, who was making a similar motion, to memorize it when he had a chance with his own chert.

"Does he have to watch us?" Powaw asked Nootau.

Nootau gave Atlatl a small frown. "You've already begged for as much stone as we can spare for you."

"I have something I wanted to show you," Atlatl said. "A new weapon."

"Perhaps later," Nootau said, not disguising his impatience.

Atlatl doubted that later would arrive.

"I call it a throwing stick," Atlatl said. He held it up for Nootau to see.

"You throw it?" Powaw snickered.

Atlatl ignored him.

"Watch what I can do with a stone," Atlatl said to Nootau. He placed a rounded stone in the pouch, and with a quick flick of his wrist, hurled the stone far over the heads of all of the men. None looked up with any degree of curiosity, and Nootau didn't bother to track the stone with his eyes.

Nootau grunted. "How can you call that a weapon?"

"It throws stones farther than I can without the thrower," Atlatl said.

"Stones that small bounce off hides," Nootau said. "What does it matter if you hit an animal from near or far if your weapon does no damage? Even if you can kill mice or small birds with it, you can't feed a clan through the winter with that kind of game."

Before Atlatl could think of a good answer, Banti walked up to them.

"Hey!" Powaw said to Atlatl. "Show my father your dangerous weapon!"

Banti looked puzzled, and Powaw and Nootau shared the laughter of an inside joke.

Humiliating as it was to be mocked like this, Atlatl knew it would be more humiliating to walk away. Worse, his limp would be obvious and Powaw might call out another insult. So Atlatl stood there, holding his useless throwing stick, feeling his ears burn. What had he been thinking? That somehow he might impress Nootau?

In a welcome distraction, Banti knelt, picking up a piece of chert.

"I'm using that to teach Powaw the best way to work spear points," Nootau told Banti.

Nootau grabbed the stone back from Banti and expertly knocked off a single large flake. He was so precise that when he picked up the flake, it fit perfectly back into place and didn't even show a seam.

"That is so good!" Powaw said with admiration. "Nootau is the best hunter in the Clan. I want to learn to be able to do it just like that!"

"Yes," Banti said. "We are fortunate that the best hunter in the Clan is willing to teach you."

Atlatl caught the undertone in Banti's voice, and Nootau's glance in return. Then Nootau shrugged with a small smile and replied, "That's right. I'll teach him everything he knows."

"Yes, yes," Powaw said with a chuckle. "I've heard it before. Everything I know, but not half of what you know."

Nootau and Powaw shared another chuckle, while Banti gave them both a tight smile.

With their attention diverted, Atlatl decided they wouldn't notice if he left. He didn't get far enough in time, because he was still in hearing distance when Banti spoke in sneering tones.

"Nootau," Banti said in a loud voice, "is it any wonder you spend time teaching my son these skills when your own son is more suited to work with the women?"

Atlatl told himself that Banti was saying this to lash out at Nootau, but still, those words hurt as deeply as if Banti had used a cutting stone across Atlatl's skin.

Chapter Nine

"We both know how important it is for our harmony to be turthful within the clan," Wawetseka said to Atlatl. "So why have you lied to me?"

It was another pleasant day. Since the return of the men, and the celebration that came with it, time had passed in an enjoyable routine of warm days and nights. Occasionally a stronger breeze blew, hinting at the coming cold.

Behind them at camp, there was laughter and songs among the women. They were nearly finished scraping the skin and smoking the last strips of the meat of a giant sloth that the hunters had found. The animal had been so huge it had taken many, many hours to fully butcher it.

The laughter and songs, however, were a bitter reminder to Atlatl of how his knee had slowed him so badly that he had not arrived in the trees until long after the sloth had been trapped in a net and killed. Since then, each night at the campfire, Atlatl had endured the Elders praising Powaw for his boldness with a spear thrust that all agreed was the fatal one. Even though the prey had been helpless in the net and there was no danger to Powaw, the Elders wanted Powaw to gain confidence as a hunter, for he would be joining them on expeditions after winter camp.

"Lied to you?" Atlatl felt his throat tighten. He adored Wawetseka. She was the mother to him that he did not have. She was the wisest and most respected person in the Clan. When she added steel to her voice, even her sons, Banti and Nootau, showed fear, and they were the leaders of all the Clan.

Lied to her? Did she somehow know Atlatl had been secretly feeding Cub minnows, hoping nobody would notice that Cub was well beyond the need to suckle?

In his nervousness, he reached down and scratched the top of Cub's head, who was pressing against his leg. Cub was taller, as large now as the mother dog that had suckled him.

"Yes," Wawetseka said. "You have lied to me about the river."

Now Atlatl was puzzled. There had been many, many sunsets and sunrises since the men had returned from their expedition to find Precious Stone. Since then, it had been the Healer's task to examine the marker stone in the river. Each day since his return, Banti had assured Wawetseka that the river had not risen.

"The river?"

"Listen carefully," Wawetseka said to Atlatl.

Atlatl waited for her to admonish him further. Instead, she remained silent.

"What do you hear?" Wawetseka asked.

"I'm still waiting for what you have to say to me about the river," Atlatl said.

"It is not what *I* have to say," she said. "Let the river speak to you."

Atlatl cocked his head, listening.

"What do you hear?" Wawetseka asked again.

"Water."

"Has this water risen above the marker stone?"

"No," Atlatl said with a clear conscience. "Every day the water touches the same notch on the marker stone."

It had seemed to rise before the return of the men, but after since the return of the hunters, it had stopped rising. Day after day, Wawetseka had sent Atlatl down to the river in secret to inspect the marker stone. And day after day, Atlatl had told her that the river was the same level.

"If you are not lying to me," Wawetseka said, "then the marker stone lies to you. You let it deceive you because you do not fear the river. But I do fear it. I listen to it. It sounds different. It sounds angry. Go down to the marker stone. Look closely. Do not let it deceive you. Come back and tell me what you see."

"Now?"

"Now. I will wait."

With Cub beside him, Atlatl took the path down to the river. He squatted beside the marker stone. He saw that the water level was lower on the marker stone's notch than the day before. Perhaps the river was angry because it was losing water?

As he straightened, he saw another stone. The day before, he'd laughed because this stone looked like it had a nose, and this nose stone had been at the water's edge beside the marker stone. Now the nose stone was below the water. And the marker stone was farther away, closer to the bank.

This was a mystery. Had the water moved the marker stone away from the nose stone, higher up on the shoreline of the river?

Atlatl hurried back to Wawetseka as fast as his leg would allow him. Cub stayed close. She was right where he had left her on the upper bank.

"The river *has* changed," Atlatl said. He explained that somehow the water had moved the marker stone.

"The Clan must be warned," Wawetseka said.

"Why do you fear the river so much?" Atlatl asked.

"Someday, if you become Healer, you must watch for the Turtle's first struggles against the binding that holds him. You must maintain the tradition of placing a marker stone whenever the Clan makes camp near a river. Tell me you know the story."

"We are in the Valley of the Turtle. The Turtle god has been bound and thrown in a great lake behind Ghost Mountain at the head of the valley. But he will always try to escape and flood the earth again."

"Then you should understand," Wawetseka said. "Because of the Turtle god, I fear the river."

Atlatl loved his grandmother. He loved her stories. He loved thinking about his own mother telling such stories. But he sometimes had his doubts.

"Nootau says stories about the gods aren't real," Atlatl said. "He says if I ask at the Gathering, I will find hunters who have seen Ghost Mountain. He says it is not a place of the gods, but a world of ice from where the sun rises to where the sun sets, and this world of ice continues to the end of the earth."

"You think I haven't heard that too? Yes, from Ghost Mountain, snow reaches out across land that is barren of plants and animals. There are no trees for fire and no food. This tells me the gods have made it that way to keep humans from their world. Only spirits of the dead visit and climb Ghost Mountain to the clouds above it."

Nootau had explained to Atlatl that it only appeared as if spirits were climbing upward, but these were the same spirits that came from a man's mouth as he breathed on cold winter days. Before Atlatl could make this argument, Wawetseka continued.

"I cannot change what your father chooses to believe," she said. "But I have learned that it is not the details that matter in a story, but the truth the story holds. The story tells us that Ghost Mountain is the end of our world and only gods live beyond it. Men tell us the world beyond Ghost Mountain is snow and ice and nothing more—again, the end of the world that we know. Whether you see it with your eyes or hear it in a story, the truth is the same. So we must believe that the Turtle god's wrath is real too. This is why the Elders of each generation pass stories down to the next. When

I am gone, you, in turn, must always remember that the Turtle god can destroy the world. You, in turn, must ensure that near the rivers, someone always watches a marker stone for the rising of the water. The Turtle god is an angry god, and if given a chance, will try to destroy the Clan."

She placed a hand upon Atlatl's shoulder. "Promise you will not turn your back on the stories of the Clan. Your father, we both know, believes only what he can see. As for Banti, he knows that stories give him power as the Healer, but I fear he does not believe them either."

Atlatl touched her hand. "I will not turn my back on the stories."

Wawetseka patted his hand in return. "Enough of this. Tell me about Cub. Does it still need milk?"

How badly Atlatl wanted to lie to his grandmother. He struggled to force the lie to come from his mouth.

"No," he finally said. Cub's fangs were much longer now, clearly visible jutting out of the sides of his mouth.

"As I thought," she said. "And you remember that it was your duty to set it free in the hills after it has suckled?"

"Yes," he said with the same reluctance. Cub remained against his leg. Would this be the last day the two of them would be together?

"If you remember the judgement I made," Wawetseka said, "also remember I did not declare how *soon* you had to set it free after it was beyond suckling."

"Wawetseka?"

"It seems that Cub, as you call him, no longer draws attention. I see no reason that he needs to leave the Clan just yet. But be careful. Not everyone will be happy to share our camp with a predator."

Chapter Ten

Many more sunsets and sunrises passed, bringing the first frosts of the season in the morning and rains in the day. The air was cooler, and all in the Clan knew that soon there would be rain again, perhaps with snow.

Among most in the Clan, the promise of winter also brought anticipation of the Gathering of Clans. It was only another moon cycle away. For Atlatl, however, the Gathering was yet another reminder that he would never be accepted as a hunter. He preferred his own company.

It was not unusual, then, that, midway through morning, Atlatl was alone with Cub, near the marker stone at the river's edge. The water had risen again from the day before, this time about the height of a spear tip. To pass time, Atlatl had used most of the morning to work on his stone thrower. He was amusing himself by experimenting with how far he could throw small rocks with it, watching them splash far upstream.

From the corner of his eye, Atlatl saw movement. He glanced to the top of the bank where he saw Powaw marching toward him with Apisi at his side. Powaw carried a spear. Apisi had a length of rope made from braided leather strips. "There's the thief!"

It was Powaw's voice, as angry as it was accusing. It was a tone of suppressed violence that made Cub growl in response.

"I'm no thief," Atlatl said.

"The Elders will decide," Powaw said. He pointed his spear at Cub. "You are responsible for this animal, and we saw it steal meat from a drying rack."

"Not possible. Cub is always with me," Atlatl said.

"Apisi saw it happen," Powaw said.

Atlatl turned to the small boy. "When?"

"This morning," Apisi said. He did not make eye contact with Atlatl.

"Who else saw this?" Atlatl asked. The drying rack was near the tents. If Cub had somehow sneaked away, surely there would be other witnesses.

Apisi shrugged an answer.

"I saw it too," Powaw said. "Apisi and I were together when it happened. Cub tore a strip from the rack and ran away to eat it."

Atlatl paused. Any accusation needed two witnesses. Powaw was a better liar than Apisi, but even so, the Elders would have no choice but to take action if they both said they had seen Cub steal the food.

"Have you told this to an Elder?" Atlatl asked finally. He needed time to think about how to protect Cub.

"As soon as we take Cub back to camp," Powaw answered, his spear still pointed at Cub. "Apisi, tie the rope around the animal's neck."

"No." Atlatl stepped in front of Cub.

Cub pushed his head forward and looked upward at Powaw from between Atlatl's legs. He continued to growl in a low tone.

"Apisi," Powaw said. "Do it now."

"You are threatening me with a spear," Atlatl said. "The Elders will hear of this too."

"*You* don't have a witness." He grinned and jabbed the spear at Atlatl's chest, stopping just short with each jab. "Do you see anything, Apisi? Do you see anyone threatening Atlatl?"

"No," Apisi answered. He shifted uncomfortably.

"What do you see?" Powaw asked the little boy.

Apisi said, "Only an animal that stole food from the Clan."

"This animal?" Powaw asked. "Hiding between Atlatl's legs?"

Powaw reversed his spear and prodded Cub's nose with the butt of the spear.

Atlatl's frustration and anger had been building. His explosion of rage felt like a flash of lightning, and he reacted without thinking. He grabbed the shaft of the spear with both hands and yanked it in a twisting motion.

At the same time, Cub snarled and leaped upward. He raked his claws against Powaw's forearms.

Powaw screamed and released the spear, but lost his balance, falling onto his back.

Cub pounced onto Powaw's chest.

Powaw shrieked louder and pushed Cub upward, trying to keep the large fangs away from his neck.

Atlatl hurled the spear to the side and reached down and wrapped his arms around Cub's ribs and pulled.

Cub was far heavier than Atlatl expected. Still, he was able to straighten with the animal in his arms. Cub clawed at empty air, still snarling.

Powaw scrambled backward, now bawling like a little boy.

"Apisi, you saw it!" Powaw cried. Blood streamed down his forearms. "You saw it! They both attacked me. You saw it."

A deeper voice reached them. "I saw it too."

It was Banti. He moved in slow steps down the path to put an arm around Powaw's shoulder, leaning forward as if he were in some kind of pain. His skin was tight across his face. Although he and Nootau had been born only a summer apart, Banti looked much older. "Atlatl, there will be punishment. You won't be able to hide behind your father or grandmother now."

Chapter Eleven

"You are about to face the Council of Elders," Wawetseka told Atlatl. "Attacking someone in the Clan is a grave offense and you know it."

Light from the campfire beyond them threw flickers of shadows across her face.

Atlatl had spent all day dreading darkness and the fire, when the Council of Elders would gather around it to make a ruling on the attack.

Earlier, Atlatl been forced to tie Cub to a tree near the campfire. To stop him from biting through the rope, Atlatl had tied a strip of leather around his muzzle. Cub had pawed against the leather, but his protruded fangs made it impossible for him to slip it loose.

Then Cub had screeched with anger through his closed teeth and had pulled against the rope again and again, almost to the point of strangulation, until he was too exhausted to keep fighting. Now he was curled in a ball at the base of the tree, almost invisible in the gloom beyond the campfire.

"I am listening," Atlatl said, head down. A small breeze lifted his hair, bringing the smell of smoke from the fire behind him.

"I don't think it was an accident that Banti happened to arrive at the same time that you attacked Powaw," Wawetseka said. "Think of the decision your father now faces as leader of the Clan."

Atlatl lifted his head as guilt flooded him, along with bitterness at his own stupidity. Nootau was in a difficult place. If he tried to sway Council to protect his own son, he would be accused of favoritism and bad leadership. If he voted with Council to punish his son, he would look weak for having an undisciplined son. As always, Atlatl was a disappointment to his father.

"You are not innocent," Wawetseka said. Her sadness was plain and added to Atlatl's own grief.

"I am not," Atlatl said. "I did strike out at Powaw."

"Not just that," she answered. "You have deeper questions to ask of yourself. Why is it that Powaw is so hateful to you?"

"Because of the bad blood between Banti and my own father," Atlatl answered.

"The quickness of your reply shows you give this little thought. Have you examined what it is you do that makes Powaw feel inferior to you?"

"Inferior?" Atlatl snorted. "I am the one with the damaged leg. He dances around me as I struggle to walk. It's been like that for as long as I can remember. He will become a man accepted as a hunter. I will not."

"Or perhaps that is his way of striking back at you for how *you* dance around *him* with your jokes and your stories and your tricks and how you cripple him with words. You have more intelligence than he does, and everyone in the Clan knows it, including Powaw. You have the brains and heart to rise above his mocking and choose to try to make him a friend, but instead, you constantly provoke him and make him an enemy. Just as it takes two people to build a friendship, it takes two people to stoke hatred."

Atlatl had no answer for this.

Wawetseka broke the silence. "I have had this conversation before. With Banti, when he was your age. Your father, like Powaw, is strong and well suited to hunting. Banti has never had the courage to face a mammoth with a spear, so he finds ways to weaken your father: Banti can always win an argument and twist words to his advantage. Together, their strengths could hold the Clan together. But their constant fighting puts the Clan in danger."

She placed a withered hand on Atlatl's shoulders. "If we survive long enough that you become Healer one day, perhaps you will remember that and work with Powaw to help the Clan."

"Survive long enough?" Atlatl said.

"I fear the river," Wawetseka said. "The way it continues to rise does not feel natural. I fear this valley because of it. But I cannot get your father to listen to me."

She removed her hand. "I hope it is only the fears of an old woman. First you must face the Elders. Go now, before they call for you. Show courage, even if you don't feel it."

➤

The Elders—Nootau and Banti centered among them—were seated on one side of the fire. The rest of the Clan faced them from the other side of the fire. Between them, standing with his arms at his side, Atlatl faced the Elders from the side of the fire, close enough to feel the heat. His leg ached, but he refused to lean on his good leg. He forced himself to focus on the pain of his leg. That kept him from trembling. He wondered if he would even be able to speak when the Elders finally called upon him.

Banti stood. He spent a few moments coughing, and after he had recovered his breath, he asked permission to speak to the entire Clan.

One of the Elders rose.

"The Clan survives because it adapts to new situations," the old man said. "You are Healer. We trust that you have a good reason to break with the traditions of a meeting of the Council."

"I have good reason to speak," Banti said. He coughed again. It was a dry, painful-sounding cough. "Earlier, one of the women came to me and to Nootau in private. She, too, witnessed what happened between Powaw and Atlatl. I know now that Atlatl's attack on Powaw was not unprovoked. Powaw has since admitted to me that he is as much to blame as Atlatl for what happened today. Both will learn from it. I speak as Powaw's father, then, not as Healer. For the sake of both Powaw and Atlatl, I request that the Council let this matter rest."

Thoughts were like a swirling wind in Atlatl's mind. Who was the witness? Why was Banti making peace like this?

Nootau rose. "I, too, speak as a father. My son requires discipline. I request of the Elders that I be permitted to discipline my son as a father, not as a leader of the Clan."

Atlatl expected that now there would be whispered discussion among the Elders. Instead, another old man rose and spoke. "Make it so. Council need not continue with this matter. Each of you disciplines your son as father."

The Elder sat.

"As for the saber-tooth," Nootau said, "two witnesses claim that the animal stole food from the Clan. Also, it attacked Powaw. These are grave offenses. The animal must be killed."

The first Elder stood. "Make it so. Atlatl must execute the animal."

Atlatl had expected this, but the impact still came like the blow of a stone hammer. How could he do this? How could he hold Cub and draw the razor edge of sharpened stone across the trusting animal's throat?

Because he'd expected this, he'd prepared the only argument he could think of to save Cub's life.

Atlatl stepped forward. He heard murmurs. No one had expected this.

"Step back!" Nootau ordered.

"Not so fast," Banti said. "Doesn't the accused have a right to speak? At the very least, this should be interesting."

"He may speak," said the nearest Elder.

Atlatl almost decided to shake his head and sit again, in silence. He knew he was directly disobeying his father, in front of the entire Clan. He thought of how Cub trusted him. He also thought of his father helping Powaw chip spear points and ignoring him at the edge of the circle.

Anger flared, and Atlatl chose Cub over his father. He remained standing.

"Yes?" said the nearest Elder.

"We are judging this animal as a member of the Clan," Atlatl said. "Is this not true?"

"Yes," the same Elder answered.

"Council has never demanded execution of a Clan member caught stealing," Atlatl said. "The harshest punishment for theft has only ever been banishment, not execution. If we are to judge the animal as a member of the Clan, we must punish it as a member of the Clan. Banishment, not execution."

There was silence, broken only by the crackling of the wood in the fire.

Nootau looked surprised, almost betrayed.

Banti spoke first, his voice a wheeze. "I agree with Atlatl. It should be banishment, not execution. A true leader of the Clan would say that justice is not justice unless it is applied to all members of the Clan. Nootau, would you agree?"

"Justice for all," Nootau finally said in a dull voice. He had no choice, Atlatl realized: if he disagreed, it would look like he didn't care about being just.

Atlatl did not dare make eye contact.

The Elders began to whisper among themselves.

Atlatl had not expected help from Banti, and he couldn't help but feel wary. But he allowed himself to hope. Banishment would be no different than what Wawetseka had already decreed. Could it be possible?

Finally, the first Elder stood.

"Atlatl speaks truth," the Elder said. "By accepting this animal among us, it became part of the Clan. Justice is not justice unless it is applied in the same way to all members of the Clan. The animal shall be banished, not executed."

Mixed with Atlatl's relief for Cub was his deep regret at how he had diminished his father in front of the entire Clan.

Chapter Twelve

*I*n the morning, Atlatl again faced the Clan. He carried his spear, and his tool kit was strapped to his waist: the normal preparation for an expedition away from camp. But this would not be a normal expedition, for the Clan had gathered to watch him take Cub into banishment, where no one would ever be permitted to provide food or shelter for him. No member, including Atlatl, would be permitted to speak to or about him. No songs of mourning would be chanted in memory of Cub. It would be as if he had never walked the earth.

As Atlatl approached Cub, who was still tied to the tree, he wanted to keep his head down and pretend no one was there. Yet he took the advice that Wawetseka had given him at dawn.

Face all of them. In a matter of days, you will be forgiven for your actions because many of them have sympathy for you. But if you show shame, that will never be forgotten.

With an expressionless face, Atlatl stopped and made a point of looking into the eyes of each Clan member.

The Elders gave him impassive stares in return.

Some of the others flinched, some turned away.

Powaw smirked. Banti gave him a nod.

Takhi smiled encouragingly. Any other time, this would have brightened his day.

Atlatl looked beyond Takhi to find his father, but did not see Nootau among the Clan members. This felt like a spear thrust into his belly.

As Atlatl untied the rope, Cub rubbed against his leg. This, too, felt like a spear thrust into his belly.

When the rope was free of the tree trunk, Cub took a step, as if expecting to be completely free of the rope. But Atlatl kept hold of one end, and Cub snarled when it pulled at his neck. Atlatl saw blood on the fur of Cub's neck where the noose had been tight and knew he was snarling from pain and frustration.

Atlatl knelt in front of Cub. He untied the leather that had bound Cub's jaw. If anyone had expected Cub to snap his teeth on Atlatl's arm, they were disappointed. Instead, Cub rubbed his muzzle against Atlatl's hand.

"Cub," he whispered. "Stay with me."

Holding the rope to guide Cub, Atlatl walked past the members of the Clan, grateful that Cub stayed at his side like Cub always did, as if the rope was not there to bind them together.

As he passed the watching eyes of each of the Clan members, Atlatl kept his shoulders straight and square, showing courage that he did not feel.

With sunlight in his face, he led Cub up the path and away from camp, along the river. There was only one place Cub belonged. Atlatl had decided to release Cub at the den where the two of them had first escaped the dire wolves.

As soon as Atlatl was high enough into the hills to be out of sight of the Clan, he untied the rope from Cub's neck. He loosely wrapped the rope in a circle over his shoulder.

When Atlatl resumed walking, Cub followed. Of all the things that hurt Atlatl's heart that morning, this loyalty was the worst.

➤

Outside the den near the top of the hill that overlooked the valley, not even scattered bones remained of the mother saber-tooth. A pair of tiny birds flitted from branch to branch on a tree sticking out from the gully wall. A downward breeze carried through the gully.

Atlatl sat on a large rounded stone and watched as Cub explored the crevices.

The animal's shoulders were becoming massive, and Cub swung from side to side with the relaxed movement of an adult. It occurred to Atlatl that if Cub decided to attack, the animal was big enough that Atlatl would not survive without a weapon to defend himself.

Yes, he told himself, Cub was ready to survive without him. It was time to say goodbye.

Atlatl stood, and Cub tracked Atlatl's new movement with his eyes. The animal trotted toward Atlatl.

"Go away," Atlatl told Cub. "I never liked you anyway. All you did was follow me around and trip my feet. You never laughed at my stories either."

The animal rubbed against Atlatl's good leg. Atlatl couldn't help himself. He dropped his hand and scratched the top of Cub's head.

"You could make this easy on me," Atlatl said. "Go look for food."

Cub stayed at his side.

Atlatl had dreaded this moment. Now that it was here, he realized that he needed to find a way to make sure Cub didn't follow him.

He pushed Cub away.

Cub made a playful pounce back to Atlatl.

He reversed his spear and prodded Cub to go back.

Cub swatted at the spear shaft, easily pushing it aside.

"Go!" Atlatl shouted. "Go!"

He realized that he was crying.

"Please go," he sobbed. "Please."

Atlatl turned and ran away as best as he could on his damaged leg. Within a flash, Cub was beside him.

He stopped. Cub stopped.

Atlatl's frustration rose. He lifted the spear, ready to hit Cub's rear haunches with the side of the spear shaft. Surely that would drive him away.

Yet Atlatl couldn't force himself to strike. He fought a couple more sobs, then knelt and hugged Cub.

"You are banished," Atlatl whispered to the animal. "Don't you understand?"

He felt a rumble of contentment from Cub.

To dry his tears, Atlatl wiped his face against the animal's fur.

He pushed away from Cub and returned to the rounded rock to think. It seemed there was only one thing he could do.

He stood and limped toward the nearest tree.

Cub followed.

Atlatl tied one end of the rope around the trunk. He made the other end into a noose.

"I'm so sorry," Atlatl told Cub.

He winced again at the sight of the raw wounds around Cub's neck where the animal had pulled against the rope earlier, but he saw no choice.

He slipped the noose over Cub's neck and stepped back.

Cub followed, then screeched at the pressure of the rope.

"You can't follow," Atlatl said. "You are banished. Please understand."

Sobbing again, Atlatl took his spear and limped away from Cub.

Cub began to yowl.

Atlatl dared not look back.

He had not muzzled the animal. Soon enough, Cub would bite through the rope to free himself. By then, Atlatl would be long gone.

Chapter Thirteen

The following morning, Atlatl held Wawetseka's right elbow as she walked toward the men of the Clan. They sat in their rough circle at the edge of the upper bank, laughing at jokes as they enjoyed their camaraderie. All of them were flaking new tools from the Precious Stone carried back from their expedition. Dull, discarded spear points formed a pile beside them.

As Atlatl and Wawetseka approached, Nootau stood and walked toward them, his shoulders rigid with suppressed anger. "I am in no mood for any kind of talk."

Nootau had not spoken a word to Atlatl since the Council of Elders.

"Nootau," Wawetseka said, "as Clan leader, you must make the decision for all of us to move this camp away from the river."

"Only when the winter has ended," Nootau said.

"This valley is rich with game to hunt; it is well protected from the winds. Aside from our journey to the Gathering and back, we stay here until the snow is gone."

"Your rivalry with your brother puts us in danger. Because this is such a good place to winter, he does not want to declare that the river is rising. He would rather hide it from the Clan than warn us to move and lose support to you when the grumblings begin at leaving behind this valley."

"The river does not rise," Nootau answered. "Banti measures it against the marker stone."

"He moves the marker stone to make it appear that way," Wawetseka said. "Ask Atlatl if that is true."

Nootau gave Atlatl a questioning look. Atlatl nodded. Each morning since Wawetseka had asked Atlatl to listen to the river, he'd found a place to watch in secret to observe Banti doing it.

Wawetseka said, "You must be the one to confront Banti over this. If I speak to Banti on behalf of the Clan, it makes you look weak."

"If I direct Banti to send us away from this valley just as winter is coming, I'm the one who loses the support of the Clan."

"You are thinking as a man who puts his rivalry ahead of the Clan."

"I am thinking as a man who needs to ensure the Clan survives winter." Nootau crossed his arms. "Stories are just stories. Water levels change all the time. As leader of the Clan, I forbid you to talk of the rising river. There is no reason to stir up unnecessary fear. Do you understand? We have found a good, safe place to stay. That is my final word on this matter."

➤

That afternoon, in pleasant sunshine, Atlatl crept from one tree trunk to another. He did his best to move from shadow to shadow. He occasionally leaned his twisted leg against the bark of a tree as he peeked around it.

Atlatl was stalking a small bird on a low branch ahead. It flitted in unpredictable movements.

Atlatl took another sneaky step, wincing at a loud snap as he stepped on a dried broken branch. Yet, clumsy as he was, his prey seemed unconcerned.

Atlatl had a stone loaded in the leather pouch of his stone thrower. He flipped the stick backward with a cock of the wrist. He made sure that the open leather pouch faced the sky so that the stone did not drop out.

He stepped into his throw and straightened his wrist with a quick flick to snap the stick forward. The leather pouch made a cracking sound as Atlatl flung his arm forward. The stone whizzed through the air.

And . . .

A leaf above the bird popped loose as the stone plucked through it. The bird chirped and flitted to another branch as the leaf dropped.

This was his seventh unsuccessful attempt. What frustrated Atlatl most was that the bird seemed unaware of the great hunter that stalked it.

"You don't have long to live," Atlatl warned the bird.

It cheerily bounced to another branch.

A pouch hanging from Atlatl's waist held his last three stones. When these were gone, he'd have to return to the riverbank and find another handful.

Despite what he had said to the bird, Atlatl actually wondered if there was any point in wasting more time. He had not once come close to hitting it. He sighed in frustration and grabbed the last three stones from his pouch, ready to just toss them on the ground and head back to camp.

He looked down at the stones in his hand.

Three stones at once?

Hmmm.

The stones were too big to be thrown at the same time.

But what if he tried pebbles? A handful of pebbles from his throwing stick, launching in a wide circle. All it would take was one of those pebbles to hit the bird . . .

Atlatl turned and hobbled toward the riverbank.

Chapter Fourteen

Atlatl sat on the large round stone in front of the den where he'd abandoned Cub four days earlier. He had his spear propped beside him, and the stone thrower was nearby. Now—unlike when Atlatl stalked the birds—it was time for an ambush. He needed to be still and patient, waiting for his prey to approach. He hoped it would be Cub.

Ahead of him—on the ground between the rock where he sat and the den where Cub had been born— were the six dead and bloodied birds he had just placed out as bait. These were proof of his stealth and patience as a hunter. The bodies were proof, too, that the stone thrower was a capable weapon when he used a handful of small stones: the stones flew in a large circle that demanded less accuracy than a single larger stone.

He'd already spent the previous three afternoons trying the same ambush. Each of the three afternoons, Atlatl had left the birds behind after waiting hours for prey that never turned up. Upon each return, he'd found scattered feathers and bones to show that an animal had scavenged the tiny bodies.

But was this scavenger the animal he was trying to ambush? Was it Cub? Or had Cub died or disappeared, and was it another animal eating the birds that Atlatl brought?

The only way he'd get the answer was by waiting.

He cocked his head to listen. He wanted to call out for Cub, but didn't want to draw in any predators, like the dire wolves they had faced before.

Atlatl heard a distant rumble come from dark clouds at the horizon far up the valley. He couldn't help but glance upward to see if a thunderbird was riding the air.

He blinked. Far away, a dot against the sky soared upward.

He strained his vision. It did appear large. But to actually believe it was a thunderbird seemed silly. It was too far away, and there was nothing to give Atlatl a comparison of size. It would be even sillier to attempt to tell anyone in the Clan that he'd seen a thunderbird. No one would believe him.

The dot faded.

More rumbling.

This troubled him. Rain upstream would only add to the height of the river. It was running fast enough now that some of the women in the Clan talked about it in low voices, but the men reassured them that the river would never reach their camp on the upper bank.

Atlatl heard something else. A stirring of bushes somewhere behind him.

His skin tingled. Was something stalking him?

Or was it Cub, finally approaching?

With heightened awareness, Atlatl focused on hearing the sound again. A long-enough time passed without the noise that he began to relax.

Faint rumbling continued from the dark and distant clouds.

Atlatl stood and stretched, grimacing at the pain from his damaged leg.

Then, as Atlatl settled back to sit on the large stone, he saw a patch of brown-orange fur through a screen of branches down the gully.

Atlatl froze.

Saber-tooth!

He saw another flash of the brown-orange fur. Atlatl's skin tingled at a sudden thought. This animal was moving like a hunter stalking prey.

What if it was a different saber-tooth?

Atlatl stood again, spear at the ready.

It was obvious that this animal knew of Atlatl's presence, so there was no harm in finally calling out.

"Cub?"

A growl came as a return answer.

Not a threatening growl. But one of acknowledgment.

The animal burst out from behind the branches and scampered toward him.

"Cub!"

Cub stopped well short of Atlatl.

Atlatl stepped toward him.

Cub backed away an equal distance.

"I have no rope," Atlatl said. Not with him. He'd left it hidden in trees behind him, hoping Cub wouldn't try to follow him back to camp.

He was also taking another risk. Banishment meant that no one from the Clan was permitted to make contact. No food or shelter shared. No conversations. It was why banishment was the most severe punishment that the Council of Elders could impose.

But Atlatl had not been able to stop wondering whether Cub was still alive.

With the end of his spear, Atlatl pushed one of the dead birds toward Cub. There was a hiss and a flash of motion. Cub struck, dragging the bird to a safe distance from Atlatl.

Atlatl grinned at the enthusiastic crunching of bones that followed.

Atlatl pushed another one forward. Cub flattened his body as he approached the bird—as if this was a real hunt.

Again, a hiss and flash of motion. Again, crunching of bones.

"Well, my little friend," Atlatl said. "It is good to see you. Tomorrow, I'll bring you more food."

Atlatl was proud of himself for the effectiveness of his throwing stick. Small birds were hardly worth the effort to pluck and remove the entrails for roasting, so he didn't expect the Clan would celebrate it as a new weapon for men to use on real hunts. Yet it was so much easier to kill birds with the throwing stick than to use a net . . .

Cub's tail twitched as he prepared to pounce on the third bird. Small feathers stuck to the side of his mouth.

Atlatl laughed.

Cub paused and growled at him.

"So," Atlatl said to Cub, "in your language, this is how you thank someone?"

"No," came a voice. "In our language, this is how I go back to the Clan and tell the Elders that you have broken the law of banishment."

Atlatl turned.

Coming toward him, from the direction of the bushes where he had heard the rustling, were Powaw and Apisi.

Two witnesses.

"You see?" Powaw told Apisi with a triumphant grin. "My father was right that Atlatl would choose this animal over the laws of the Clan. All we had to do was follow him until it happened."

Atlatl felt the blood leave his face. It had all been a trap. Banti had asked the Elders for banishment, guessing that Atlatl would come after Cub. Atlatl could not begin to guess what price he would pay for this.

Chapter Fifteen

"I stand before you as leader of this Clan," Nootau said to the Elders. "And I speak to you as leader of this Clan, not as father of Atlatl."

These were the first words spoken to the Elders at the fire. As before, the Elders were gathered on one side, and the remainder of the Clan on the other. Atlatl stood to the side. He barely noticed the sting of sleet driven by a cold wind as the afternoon's distant storm began to sweep through this part of the valley.

Banti rose and spoke with outrage. He had wrapped himself in an animal skin. "And I speak as Healer. I—"

He had to stop briefly at a wheezing cough. When he resumed, he didn't sound as vigorous. "I request that the Elders acknowledge that Nootau is no longer suitable to lead the Clan or even address the Elders. His son betrays us and angers the gods."

"My son—" Nootau began, but Banti cut him off, speaking to the Elders as if Nootau did not exist.

"His son brought a predator among us, a predator that attacked a member of the Clan." Banti coughed, but only briefly. "Nootau's son broke the laws of the Clan. We cannot let this divide us. The Clan must be united to survive. With Nootau as leader, we are divided. With Nootau as leader, the gods show their anger by raising the river. If we are forced to leave this camp, it is because of Nootau and Atlatl."

"My son—" Nootau tried again, but this time, one of the Elders interrupted.

"Your son disregarded the decree of the banishment," the Elder told Nootau. "Do you dispute that?"

"I do not," Nootau answered.

"Then if you are to remain leader of this Clan, you understand what is required of you."

Atlatl shivered, but not because of the cold. The Elder was telling Nootau to declare that Atlatl must be punished by banishment too.

Nootau bowed his head. Wind plucked at the furs that wrapped him. For long moments, Nootau did not move.

Atlatl bowed his own head. He had no one to blame but himself. It wasn't loneliness or death that he feared, as much as the grief he felt over the pain he was causing his father.

"You are asking me to send my own son away." Nootau bowed his head again, then lifted it to try one more time to speak.

He could not do this to his father. Atlatl stepped forward. "I banish myself."

Murmuring came from the others in the Clan.

One of the Elders rose and shook a fist at him. "Do not show disrespect for the rulings of the Elders. This is not a choice you can make."

Atlatl drew a breath to defy the Elder. After all, how much worse could this be? Whether he was banished by his own father or he banished himself, he would no longer be able to live among the Clan. What did it matter if he infuriated the Elders?

He felt a hand on his shoulder and heard a soft voice.

"This is not your battle," Wawetseka said. "All along it has been between your father and his brother. So hold your silence."

She kissed Atlatl on the forehead. She patted Nootau's shoulder. Then she took her position in front of the Elders.

"No man should be forced to decide what you are asking Nootau to decide," she began. "No man should have to choose between the survival of the Clan or the survival of his son. As the oldest member of the Clan, my advice to the Elders is to first remove Nootau as leader and declare that Banti take his place. Then we will trust Banti and the Elders to make a just decision in regard to Atlatl."

One of the Elders rose. "This is wise. We will speak among ourselves."

Wawetseka nodded and remained where she was as the Elders talked in low voices. Frail as Wawetseka was, she seemed as solid as a mountain, even as the wind picked up in strength.

The discussion did not take long.

"We have decided. Banti will be the Clan's leader."

In the firelight, Atlatl saw the gleam of Banti's teeth as the man smiled in triumph. Because Banti's face was skeletal thin, he seemed like a wolf as he smiled.

All along, Banti had been using Atlatl to make this happen. And Atlatl had walked right into the trap.

"Now," Wawetseka said, "before the Elders decide on the punishment for Atlatl, I will speak to the leader of the Clan."

She faced Banti. "First, it is now within your power to move the Clan from this valley. Nootau ignored the marker stone because, as hunter and leader, he believed it would serve the Clan better to ignore what the gods are telling us. You are not only leader, but Healer. You serve the gods. You know that the marker stone is telling us that the Turtle god is angry. You and I have agreed upon this in private. Now make your decision in front of the Clan."

Atlatl could only marvel at Wawetseka's brilliance. Anticipating that Nootau was going to lose the leadership, she had used the opportunity to try to get Banti to act and move the Clan to higher ground.

But it was not to be.

Banti answered her almost immediately. "What we spoke of in private no longer matters now that I am leader."

He faced the Clan. "The gods do speak to us. The river did not rise until Atlatl brought the animal into the Clan. Yet I will be a merciful leader. As leader, I ask that the Elders send Nootau and Atlatl into the hills tomorrow to return to camp with the saber-tooth. On their return, to make the gods happy and keep the river from rising farther, Atlatl will sacrifice the animal with all of us to witness. If, after that, the river continues to rise because the gods are not appeased, then Atlatl will be banished."

Chapter Sixteen

*N*ootau's silent fury was obvious as he marched ahead of Atlatl upward into the gorge that held Cub's lair.

Just after dawn, with the entire Clan gathered and watching in silence, the two of them had departed from camp.

The morning sunshine was pleasant and had melted the early frost. Yet he felt no pleasure in the warmth of the day. Only misery and dread.

Misery because of how he'd led to his father's humiliation in front of the Clan. There would be no forgiveness, it seemed. Nootau had not spoken one word to Atlatl since beginning the march.

Not only had he already betrayed his father, next he would have to betray Cub.

Early, before anyone had stirred from their tents, Atlatl had used his stone thrower to kill a few small birds.

When they reached Cub's lair, Atlatl laid the body of the first bird outside of the lair and whistled. Cub leaped outside in the sunshine and rolled twice. Playful. Happy.

This only filled Atlatl with more misery.

Nootau jabbed his spear in Cub's direction and finally spoke. "Tie the animal's legs together. Then muzzle it. We carry it by the shaft of my spear."

It was how hunters transported deer they had killed. Hanging upside down from a pole.

Atlatl did not dare open his mouth in protest. It had to be done.

He patted the side of his leg, and Cub bounded over and rubbed his head against Atlatl's thigh. Atlatl reached into his tool kit for a length of leather lace to wrap around Cub's muzzle. A sudden gust of wind plucked at his hair.

The gust became a sustained wind, growing stronger.

It was strange enough that Atlatl glanced at Nootau, who was cocking his head in puzzlement. There were no clouds in the sky.

The wind gusted upward, as if coming from the direction where the river came out of a gap in the far hills. It continued to grow in strength. Atlatl's skin tingled. As if the wind were a warning.

Cub howled and scurried back to the lair.

Nootau had his spear in both hands, as if ready for battle. But there was no enemy visible.

Then a shout as Takhi rushed into the narrow part of the gorge.

Takhi?

She gasped out her words, pointing down the hill. "The Clan! The river! We have to flee!"

"The river?" Nootau asked.

"It's reached the upper bank. The water is still rising! Come with me. Hurry! They won't wait for us if we are late. They can't."

The wind continued to grow. It came with a low rumbling sound.

Another shout. This from Powaw, who was sprinting toward them.

"You were supposed to stay and help the children!" Takhi said.

"Banti told me to follow! Already the water is above the upper bank!"

Nootau turned and began to run back down the hill. As he disappeared from Atlatl's sight, the low rumbling sound became a roar of thunder, and the wind picked up enough power to lift Atlatl's hair. He blinked in disbelief.

Takhi brought her hands to her mouth in the same

disbelief. Powaw turned to the source of the wind and the sound.

Water.

Up the valley, it shot out from the gap in the far horizon where the valley walls opened for the river. It was a towering wall as high as the tops of the hills. The water burst through the gap and surged forward, blowing out massive pieces of the hills that tumbled and disappeared into the raging waters.

Atlatl could not find words. What he was seeing was beyond comprehension. The wall of water was as large as any mountain.

The thunderous sound continued as the water surged. It entered the open valley and widened. Yet even as it filled the valley, the water coming from the gap remained as high as the hills behind it, pushing air ahead of it that hit them like wind from a storm.

"The Turtle god!" Powaw wailed.

He sprinted away. Upward. Away from the approaching water.

Atlatl was high enough up this hill to see that if it continued to roar out from between the narrow hills at this speed, the rushing water would cross a half day of walking distance in minutes and wash them away like they were mere chips of wood.

He thought of the Clan. If they were still down at the upper riverbank, they wouldn't be able to see to the horizon like Atlatl. Nor would Nootau, who was already gone. They would hear the sound but would be unaware of the mountain of water behind it.

Atlatl began to hobble downward. To warn them.

Moments later, he was conscious of someone beside him.

Takhi. Running as hard as he was.

"No!" She had to shout to be heard over the sound of the wind and the approaching water. She tugged at his shoulder. "It's too late!"

The world was ending. The water was rising as quickly as a hawk could soar. Already, the near edge of the wall of water was close enough that Atlatl could see entire trees flipping and rolling in the water as if they, too, were mere chips of wood.

Takhi tugged at Atlatl's shoulder again. "Higher!"

They turned and fled upward into the gorge. Just as they reached it, the first wave of water splashed against their ankles. A second wave against their knees. Atlatl fell forward. The water was as cold as ice.

Takhi reached out and yanked him upward. He managed to stand, but already they were waist-deep in water and it was pushing them under.

Atlatl felt something scratch against his back. It was the branches of a huge uprooted tree, spinning on the surface of the muddy water.

"Takhi! Grab hold!"

He grasped a branch and dragged himself onto it.

Takhi went under the water.

Atlatl screamed her name.

Her hair floated on the surface, just beyond the tree.

Atlatl wrapped his legs around the branch, and lunged forward. Barely, just barely, he managed to grab her hair with his fingers. He tugged, and her head broke the surface. She sputtered and coughed.

Then awareness came into her eyes. She reached upward for a branch and pulled herself into the tree.

Something bobbed beside her.

Cub.

The saber-tooth was screeching in panic.

With his legs still wrapped around the branch, Atlatl lunged again. He grabbed Cub around his chest and dragged him closer.

The water pulled at Atlatl. He felt as if his upper body were a blade of grass, waving in the currents. Still holding Cub, Atlatl managed to turn. Water splashed into his eyes. He pushed Cub toward the thicker branches, where he clawed for safety, then leaped forward onto the trunk of the tree.

This freed Atlatl's hands, and he, too, pulled himself toward the trunk of the tree.

Above him, the sky spun. Atlatl became aware of swarms of birds of all sizes, screeching in panic, dipping and turning in flight, driven into the air by the massive and sudden flood.

He gasped. He glanced over at Takhi, who was heaving for breath.

They were safe. The tree rose with the water as the water continued to rush into the gorge. Beside them, the lower ledges of the rock walls disappeared as if eaten by water.

Then Takhi shouted again.

"It's Powaw!"

Atlatl followed her gaze. Their tree was pinched between the walls of the gorge as the water kept rising toward the top of the hill. Powaw was sprinting ahead of them, trying to reach the pinnacle. And behind, Nootau, catching up to Powaw.

But it was a race they were doomed to lose.

Chapter Seventeen

"Powaw! Powaw!" Atlatl shouted.

Holding his spear in one hand, Nootau had grabbed Powaw's hand in the other and was dragging him forward. They were almost at the tree.

Atlatl crawled out again on one of the branches of the floating tree. The end of the branch dipped into the water with his weight. He wrapped his legs around the branch again. All he needed to do was reach out far enough . . .

"Powaw!" he shouted again.

His voice reached Powaw, who turned as the water slapped against his thighs.

Powaw instantly understood that he had one hope of survival. The floating tree. But he was still too far ahead, and the rising water would sweep him away with the approach of the tree.

He grabbed a shrub sticking out of the rock wall. Water rose to his chest. Then his neck.

The tree spun closer. Then, taken away by the vagaries of the current, it spun away again.

"Powaw!" Atlatl shouted, stretching his arm out as far as he could.

He felt Powaw's fingers close on the tips of his fingers. He curled his fingers into a fist. Powaw did the same. Their grip was solid. Powaw released the shrub and the water dragged at his body.

Atlatl strained to hold tight. But Powaw was too heavy, and the bark of the tree was too slick. Atlatl's legs began to slip loose from the branch.

To save himself, Atlatl would have to uncurl his fingers and let Powaw drown.

Who could blame him if he did? Why should they both die? This was the Powaw who'd bullied him relentlessly, mocked him daily.

Yet, somehow, he could not. He heard Wawetseka's voice in his mind. Powaw was part of the Clan. Powaw was *his* Powaw. The Clan survived because its members took care of each other.

It took all his willpower to keep the grip. Water filled his nose. His ears.

Then he felt something else.

A hand had grabbed his ankle!

Tahki?

No. The grip was too strong. As he was dragged back to safety, he realized it was Nootau.

Slowly, Nootau pulled Atlatl into the branches. With Atlatl came Powaw, who clutched at the first branch he could get his hands on.

Each of them crawled back toward the trunk of the tree. They found perches in the canopy, as if they were birds. The tree was on its side, large enough that the branches spread out and kept it from rolling. Instead, the huge tree slowly spun on the surface of the water as it continued to rise. In all directions, birds circled above. Only the distant tips of the highest hills showed above the surface of the muddy brown waters.

All of them were safe. For now. Five of them. All shivering. All sitting on the trunk of the massive tree.

Nootau. Atlatl. Takhi. Powaw. And Cub.

➤

Atlatl sat upright, tool kit hanging against his chest, legs propped along the trunk of the tree, his back against a branch. For a long, long while, there were no words. For his part, Atlatl was too numb with cold and too shocked to speak. He wondered if it was the same for the others.

They had just been struck by a mountain of water! And, looking back at the gap in the valley, it kept coming and coming. How could that be?

As the afternoon sun began to dry and warm him, Atlatl tried to comprehend how the world had shifted. In all directions, the water continued to rise and push them down to the wider sections of the valley. From one side of the valley to the other, it would have been easily two days of walking, but now the water and floating debris filled it completely.

Powaw broke the silence.

"Atlatl is to blame," Powaw said. "Our Clan has been punished because he has broken the rules."

Powaw sat on the trunk farther down, near the center of the tree, with Takhi at the end of the tree where its trunk was widest at the base. In the other direction, closer to the top and huddled in a cluster of branches that formed the canopy, Cub tried unsuccessfully to crouch and hide among the water-soaked leaves. Nootau rode the trunk near the tip of the tree, holding branches to balance himself, his face unreadable.

Atlatl was too despondent to protest. Wawetseka

gone. The children gone. Washed away in this cold, cold water now as deep as the valley.

"Powaw," Atlatl said. "If we are all that remains of the Clan, we need to work together to survive."

Powaw's response was merely to grunt. Nootau remained silent.

Atlatl's thoughts turned to the story of the Turtle god. How had Turtle managed to break his bonds and wreak this havoc?

As they drifted, the current of the water slowed. The tree appeared to move backward, against the flow of the massive lake that continued to expand. Atlatl saw that the current was swirling, taking them within a stone's throw of the rocky edge that had once been the highest hills in the valley. There was an island, hardly larger than an area of encampment. It had once been the peak of the hill. Some of it was flat and grassy, and hundreds of birds were now perched on it.

One of the birds flew out to their floating tree and landed on the tip.

Cub reacted by trying to stand and swat the bird. It fluttered away with a squawk.

Suddenly, the tree seemed to be moving again. It looked like the land was rising. But Atlatl realized that, actually, the tree was dropping. Water, then, was finally flowing out of the far end of the valley.

The tree hit land and the top part settled on a ledge. The water dropped more, and the tree began to tilt upright as the base remained in the water and the upper branches rested on the ledge.

Cub sprang upward and found footing on the wet rock.

"If the water is dropping," Nootau said, "it should be safe to leave the tree. Atlatl, you are nearest. You go first. I will follow."

Nootau flung his spear ahead onto the land.

Atlatl scrambled up the trunk of the tree, following Cub's path. He pushed off the branches and splashed through shallow water to reach a higher shelf of the rocky ledge.

With his balance secure, Atlatl looked down at the tree. Nootau was already stepping onto the ledge. Atlatl expected to see Powaw following.

Instead, Powaw had stopped near the top of the tree, where a branch was stuck against the ledge and keeping the tree from floating downstream. Powaw was holding the branch with two hands and pushing his legs against the ledge, his back to Takhi, who was crawling upward along the trunk to get to the ledge.

"Powaw!" Takhi shouted.

"I'm holding on as tight as I can!" Powaw shouted. "Takhi, hurry and join them!"

Powaw's jaws were tight with effort. But it seemed to Atlatl that Powaw was using his strength to push the tree away, not hold it steady.

From land, Atlatl reached for the branches and caught one in time. The current pulled at the submerged branches of the tree, and Atlatl began to topple into the water. He felt his father's strong hand grab one of his biceps, keeping him in place. They had become a human chain—Nootau solidly on land and holding Atlatl, Atlatl with the branch in his hand, trying to keep the tree from getting washed away by the current.

"Help us!" Powaw shouted. "Don't let us go!"

Atlatl grunted with effort.

"Takhi," Powaw yelled. "He's pushing us away! He wants us to die!"

The current was too strong. Without Powaw to help by pulling, branch tips slid through Atlatl's fingers. The current yanked the tree away from the ledge.

Atlatl's eyes met Powaw's as the tree spun back into the current.

Powaw grinned in triumph.

"We will find our way to the Gathering, I promise," Powaw called out as the distance between them widened. "You are the cause of this flood. You should banish yourself and flee in the opposite direction."

Chapter Eighteen

When he and Cub climbed upward to the flattened top of the temporary island, Atlatl saw even more birds of different sizes resting on the grassy land and clustered among the branches of the small trees. Of any of the animals in the way of the flood, it made sense that birds would have been best able to avoid drowning as the water rose so quickly. They were oddly silent, as if they, too, were stunned at what had happened.

Nootau would be happy to know about this. At least they could hunt birds. Atlatl still had his throwing stick and it looked like there were plenty of stones. Perhaps now his father would see the benefit of the new weapon.

Atlatl left Cub behind and walked back down to the rocky ledge where he and Nootau had jumped from the floating tree. The water level had already dropped from where he stood on the ledge, revealing more and more of the hill it had once covered. Broken pieces of trees bobbed in the muddy waters, moving faster in the deadly current than Atlatl could run.

The tree with Powaw and Takhi was a tiny dot, following the water to where it seemed to pour out of the lower edge of the valley, slowly and with less violence. Atlatl could only hope that when the current finally took Powaw and Takhi there, they could survive the outflow of water.

Nootau was nearby and facing down the valley. Atlatl had started toward him when the movement of a monstrous dark shadow in the sky to Atlatl's right caught his attention.

For a few moments, it was a puzzling sight. Then it flapped, and Atlatl realized, impossibly, it was a bird.

He'd never seen anything that large in the air. From wing tip to wing tip, it seemed as wide as the length of a mammoth from trunk to tail.

It drifted closer with a few more flaps of its wings.

It could only be one thing. A bird not seen by anyone in the Clan since Atlatl was a young boy, a bird that some believed was just a story.

Thunderbird. Had the floodwaters driven it into the skies?

"Nootau," Atlatl called. His father needed to see this!

His father did not turn. Rigid anger showed in Nootau's shoulders and back.

The thunderbird passed directly overhead. It was so black it appeared almost purple. Atlatl could clearly see the massive curved beak, talons that each seemed as large as a grown man's fingers, and huge pinion feathers on the tips of wings curved upward to catch the wind.

"Nootau!" Perhaps his father had not heard Atlatl above the sound of the rushing water.

His father still ignored him.

Atlatl watched the thunderbird soar to the near hills of the valley. It was then that Nootau finally turned. He stared at Atlatl for a few moments.

"Nootau," Atlatl said. "You should have looked. It was a thunderbird. It . . ."

Atlatl pointed, but now the thunderbird was too far away to appear like anything but a speck in the sky.

Nootau glanced at the speck.

"Even now," Nootau said, "you tell lies."

Nootau turned away again to stare down the valley.

"It was!" Atlatl protested. "It was . . ."

Atlatl let his voice die away.

Guilt pressed upon Atlatl, and the sight of the thunderbird suddenly seemed of no importance. He deserved his father's shunning. Atlatl was alive only because of his selfishness. Selfish to keep Cub. Selfish to ignore the banishment decree.

It should have been Atlatl to die in the flood. Instead, it was the Clan who had been washed away.

His only consolation was that his selfishness had saved Powaw and Takhi and Nootau.

If Powaw and Takhi survived, they would make it to the Gathering. They would be able to join one of the other clans.

As for Atlatl? The sun was warm and not much past the high part of the day. He was on land and—while the water surrounded it—safe from predators like dire wolf or saber-tooth or cheetah. The night would not become too cold, because it was still early in the season. He would probably live in safety for a couple of days. He guessed it would take that long for all the water to empty from the valley.

Yet did it even matter that he was still alive?

He was alone. Hated by his father.

Cub approached with a bird in his mouth.

Atlatl remained where he was. Silent and despondent. Now that Cub could hunt, even he didn't need Atlatl.

Cub reached Atlatl's feet, then dropped his head and spit the bird onto the damp stone. He backed away and cocked his head, gazing up at Atlatl.

Atlatl knelt on the damp stones. He picked up the still-warm bird's body.

Cub watched him without moving.

Atlatl imagined Cub's mother bringing food back to the lair and dropping it at Cub's feet. Like Atlatl had been doing, instead of leaving Cub behind as he was supposed to.

Was this a gift?

Atlatl reached into his tool kit and found his cutting stone. He used it to strip feathers and skin away from the bird's body. He pulled the breast muscles loose and pretended to dip the chunk of bloody muscle into his mouth.

Cub cocked his head again.

Atlatl cocked his own head, the faintest of smiles on his face.

Until he heard his father's voice.

"Slit that animal's throat."

Atlatl turned to his father. Nootau gripped his spear so tight that his massive biceps bulged.

"We were sent to kill that animal," Nootau said, his voice as cold as the floodwaters. "Kill it now."

Atlatl knew his father was right. Atlatl had put Cub ahead of the Clan again and again, and it had led to all of this.

Atlatl knelt beside Cub. He pulled out the cutting stone. He'd have to hug Cub around the chest and swiftly slash Cub's throat.

But what would Cub's death accomplish now?

"Kill the animal," his father said, at the edge of restrained fury.

Atlatl could not help but feel his years and years of resentment come to a point as sharp as a spearhead.

"And then?" Atlatl asked. "You will treat me like a son? Finally, I'll have done something that you can proudly speak about to others?"

"There are no others," Nootau said. His voice was a hiss of rage. "The flood has taken them away. The flood that you caused. You have taken away my position as leader of the Clan. You have destroyed the Clan itself. There will be a Gathering, and only Powaw and Takhi will be there. To tell them how Atlatl, son of Nootau, brought the anger of the gods upon the Clan. Is this what you want me to speak about?"

Atlatl could not help himself. He choked out a sob of grief.

"Or should I speak about how you are unable to hunt and instead choose to tell stories to endear yourself to others?" Nootau continued. "Should I tell them the story about an attacking thunderbird that you use to excuse yourself? Should I speak about the games you play with words—like my brother, Banti—and how you use words to torment people around you? Should I go to the Gathering and tell other clans that my son is a trickster? A boy who wishes to become Healer and, like his uncle Banti, take advantage of those who hunt and gather food by pretending to know the will of the gods? Or should I tell those at the Gathering that if I could choose a son, it would be Powaw, someone who will grow into a hunter and protector?"

Atlatl felt another sob begin at the base of his throat. He dropped his head, not wanting his father to see his tears. He'd always wondered if this was how his father felt, but to hear it said so plainly wrenched him as badly as if his father had thrown him off a cliff.

"Maybe our Clan survived," Atlatl said. "They will go to the Gathering and—"

"This flood you unleashed," Nootau said bitterly. "Do you think that any of our Clan could have survived?"

Wawetseka, gone? Nuna, gone? Kiwi, gone? The Elders, gone? No. Somehow, they must have survived. But even as he thought the words, he knew otherwise. He choked on a sob.

"And what should you care about at the Gathering?" Nootau asked. "What part of it could you deserve? You are banished. Our Clan has three. Not four. Powaw. Takhi. And me."

"No, father. No." Anguish pulled those words from Atlatl's mouth.

"Kill the animal!" his father shouted. "Kill the animal or I will kill it for you!"

Atlatl raised his head to see Nootau take another step forward, raising his spear to hurl it at Cub.

As much as grief at hearing his father's words tore him apart, Atlatl felt a surge of anger that brought him to his feet in front of Cub.

"Stand aside," Nootau snarled.

"No," Atlatl said.

He crossed his arms and stared defiantly at his father. In that moment, he was beyond any physical pain. He wasn't sure if he was standing between Cub and the spear because he wanted to save Cub's life or if he was ready for his own life to end.

"You want to be proud of me, yet not once have you been like a father to me." Atlatl trembled as he spoke aloud thoughts that he'd tried to keep down for so long. "You want me to be a hunter, but not once have you shown me how to hunt. All you've shown me is your shame for me."

If his father hated him this much, if he was banished, if he had caused the deaths of everyone he knew and loved, why not accept death as his punishment?

"Go ahead and kill me then," Atlatl said, his voice strained. "Because I will not let you kill Cub while I am alive."

Atlatl waited for the impact of the spear point to drive into his ribs and through his chest.

For far too long, Nootau's right arm quivered with the unreleased tension of the poised spear.

Then, finally, Nootau dropped his arm.

"You," he said so quietly that Atlatl could barely hear, "are not my son."

Nootau turned away and stared back out over the water.

Chapter Nineteen

Atlatl woke the next morning in warm sunshine, with Cub asleep and curled against his ribs.

He first looked for Nootau. His father was as far away as possible on their hillside ledge, sitting, with his back turned to Atlatl. The rigidness to Nootau's shoulders had not changed, and Atlatl knew his father still seethed with silent rage.

Nootau's threat with the spear rushed back into Atlatl's memory, and he gritted his teeth against the pain of his father's complete rejection. He turned to look out over the valley and his pain was replaced with awe.

The evening before, when the sun set at the far edge of the valley, water had lapped at the edge of their ledge. Now the ledge was far above the water. The Great Flood was receding and now filled only the lower third of the valley. That so much water could still be moving through the valley after an entire night was far beyond anything Atlatl could have imagined. The dark water was still violently flowing, with entire trees bobbing in it.

Atlatl wondered if he would ever be able to find words to describe it. Wawetseka's story had been truth; it had to be. What other than the wrath of an angry god could cause this much destruction?

As for the land exposed by the drop of the massive flood, it was devastated beyond belief. As far as Atlatl could see, all of the larger trees had been torn from the hills on both sides of the valley. Most of the bushes had disappeared. The grasses were covered with dark mud. The land itself was rippled where water had washed away dirt to leave behind rock.

There would be no point in descending to where the Clan had once felt secure. There was no life remaining in this valley, no game or berries to sustain any human or animal. It would be years—if the flood did not come again—before bushes and trees returned.

Atlatl turned his attention away from the broad view of the valley to the opposite side of their ledge. Yesterday, there had been water between the ledge and the hillside of the valley, making the ledge an island. Now, in both directions at roughly eye level, a horizontal line along the hills, as straight and as vivid as a knife slash, marked how high the water had risen. Below the line was mud and exposed rock. Above it, untouched by flood, were grass and flowers and trees to the top of the valley. Farther down the valley, above the flood line, Atlatl saw deer were grazing, untroubled by the disaster. Outside of this valley, game, food and berries would exist as they did before the flood. Outside of the valley was survival.

To reach this sanctuary of grass and trees meant climbing down from the ledge into the mud and broken rock, crossing a flat stretch of mud, and then a short climb upward through mud to the portion of the hills above the waterline. The mud had the slippery sheen of animal grease. Climbing up the muddy hill would be a physical task as difficult as anything he'd ever faced.

The alternative was to wait for the mud to dry. But that could take days, days without water. Living without food was one thing, but there would be no living without water. Atlatl's mouth was already dry. It had been since the afternoon the day before that he'd had any water to drink.

Atlatl saw no choice but to make the journey. He stood, which woke Cub, who stood as well and stretched with a contented growl.

Nootau did not turn toward the sound.

All Atlatl wanted was his father's friendly hand on his shoulder, the way he'd seen Nootau do with Powaw. Then maybe he could face the difficulties that lay ahead. Instead, all he had were Nootau's words echoing in his mind.

Should I go to the Gathering and tell other clans that my son is a trickster? A boy who wishes to become Healer and, like his uncle Banti, take advantage of those who hunt and gather food by pretending to know the will of the gods? Or should I tell those at the Gathering that if I could choose a son, it would be Powaw, someone who will grow into a hunter and protector?

"Father!" he called, trying to keep his voice steady.

His father showed no reaction.

No, Nootau had made it plain. He did not want Atlatl as a son. Calling out for his father was useless, then.

"Nootau!" Atlatl tried.

Nootau remained motionless.

Atlatl turned his face away and began to weep silently. He felt his shoulders heave as sobs tore at his chest, but he could not stop himself. He felt broken. This was banishment. It was as if he didn't exist.

Atlatl took a deep breath and felt his grief turn into resolve. He dropped his hand to the top of Cub's head. He scratched the animal's fur, feeling the rumble of

Cub's satisfaction. If Atlatl was shunned, there was no point remaining on the ledge. He would leave Nootau before Nootau could leave him. Nor would he look over his shoulder to see if Nootau even cared that he was leaving. He would be strong.

Atlatl hefted his tool kit, comforting himself with the knowledge that he had the most important survival tools: a hammerstone to flake his stone points, a drilling board to make fire, and a cutting rock to strip saplings and spear points. Once he reached the grass and trees, he'd find a way to survive. With Cub.

Atlatl limped toward the side of the ledge.

He lowered his feet over the ledge. It was a near vertical drop. Once he pushed off, there would be no turning back.

He peeled the skins of his clothing off and formed a bundle that he held with both arms in front of his belly. Then, without looking back, he pushed off and slid down the mud. Any other time and place, the sensation of speed would have made him shout with delight.

The flat of the small gully rushed at him, and he barely managed to keep from falling onto his side as he hit bottom.

As he stood, Cub screeched beside him. The animal had braced on all four paws. Now he was picking up each paw and trying to shake mud loose. But each time he put the clean paw down, it became dirty again. Cub whined with frustration.

"Well, friend." Atlatl laughed. "Looks like you're going to have to keep following me if you want to get the mud off."

Atlatl used some of his leather strapping to bundle the clothing and strap it to his shoulders so he could cross the mud flat. Keeping his fur clothing on his shoulders would ensure that it didn't become caked in mud like Cub's feet.

Standing on two feet would not give him enough grip, so when Atlatl reached the opposite slope, he dropped to his hands and knees. He began to crawl up the mud. Almost immediately, he began to pant with exertion, feeling thirst like a sharp stab of pain.

His progress was slow. After some trial and error, he found the only way to stop from sliding back was to grope beneath the mud and find an edge in the unyielding rock, and then pull upward.

He was so focused, it wasn't until halfway up the slope that he realized Cub was not beside him. He looked down and saw Cub struggling to climb. Any time Cub made it upward, even a little, he would slide back down.

Atlatl reluctantly let go of the rock edge and slid back down to Cub.

He put the animal in front of him and lowered his shoulders into Cub's haunches. He pushed, and Cub moved upward. Blindly, Atlatl reached beneath the mud and found a handhold on rock. He pulled himself upward, grunting at the extra weight of Cub.

The animal floundered but stayed in position, almost riding Atlatl's shoulders. Atlatl pushed through the mud with his feet. He reached upward again and found more rock to grip. Pulling with his arms and pushing with his strong leg, he managed to shove both of them upward a little more.

Again and again he moved the two of them, pausing to gasp for breath each time. It seemed like hours were passing with nothing but this painful push and pull up the hill.

Then, suddenly, the weight left his shoulders.

Atlatl lifted his head. They had reached the grass and Cub was bounding up the hill.

Atlatl wanted to collapse and lie in the mud, enjoying the victory of his climb.

But he was only halfway to the top of the valley, and he needed to find water and a place to camp.

Atlatl crawled upward until he was completely on the grass of the hillside. His belly and legs and arms were completely covered with the wet heavy mud, and he was almost too tired to stand. But he forced himself up.

Atlatl took one trembling step up the hill, leaning on his good leg and dragging his bad leg. Another trembling step and another until he reached the top of the valley. Cub stayed at his side the entire way.

He knew he was outlined against the sky in full view of Nootau on the ledge and that gave Atlatl a certain grim satisfaction: he had not failed in that difficult climb, and Nootau had surely seen it. And his father would also see that Atlatl was turning his back on him. If Nootau didn't have a son, then Atlatl didn't have a father.

As for a destination, he could go straight ahead, away from the valley and toward the lands where the sun rose. Or he could turn to his right, which would take him in the direction of the Gathering. But he would not be welcome there—Powaw would make sure of it.

His third choice was to travel parallel to the valley, upstream to Ghost Mountain. To the land of the gods who lived beyond it, where the night sky danced and shimmered with color.

Atlatl didn't hesitate. He turned toward the land of ice. He would go to where the Turtle god had unleashed the flood, no matter how long it took.

He would face the Turtle god and demand an answer. Why had the Clan been destroyed?

Part Two

TURTLE GOD

Chapter Twenty

The climb to the top of the hill had made Atlatl so thirsty that his throat seemed filled with sand.

The only consolation he could take in his desperate need for water was that it drove away the grief and pain he felt in walking away from Nootau. Water was all that occupied his thoughts. Water to drink, water to wash away the mud that was drying on his skin.

Creeks and small rivers fed the main river of the Valley of the Turtle. He told himself if he kept walking north, he would eventually find water that fed down into the now destroyed valley. Up here, the terrain was open grasslands with occasional clusters of trees. This, at least, was a good situation. He doubted he'd have to worry about predators finding a way to ambush him— he'd see them coming.

The disadvantage was that he took the full brunt of the day's heat. Although it was fall, afternoons were hot. The sun burned from a cloudless sky, and a dry wind sucked away all moisture. Atlatl forced himself to stumble forward because he had no choice. He wondered if he would have been able to find the strength to persevere without Cub at his side.

There was another danger. It was common knowledge in the Clan that it was difficult to walk a straight line over a long distance. The tendency was to travel in a large circle. Since he might have to move far enough away from the edge of the valley to use it as a reference, Atlatl chose a point on the horizon and aimed toward that.

As he fought his thirst, Atlatl glanced at the sky to judge the passage of the sun. How long before the day ended?

Suddenly, there it was. Again. A huge soaring shadow. Thunderbird! As if it were following him. Surely it was the same one he'd seen from the ledge. Perhaps it had had a nest in the valley, a nest destroyed by the flood. Perhaps it, too, was condemned to wander without a home.

Atlatl followed the drifting of the bird until it was long out of his sight.

He pushed forward, trying to distract himself from his thirst by wondering about the thunderbird.

See, he told himself, the story about a thunderbird wasn't the imagination of a storyteller. If only they could see that I'm right. If only . . .

Atlatl caught himself. Nobody remained from the Clan. The water had washed them away. What did it matter if Atlatl had really been attacked by a thunderbird as a child? The Clan was gone—there was no one to tell.

Moments later, he realized he was singing a song of mourning. His grief seemed to sustain him, and he found the strength to keep walking.

Finally, long after the sun had reached the midpoint of the sky, they reached a gully. Cub began to trot forward, and Atlatl followed. He hobbled down into the gully behind Cub and grinned. Water! It was a shallow creek that he could have crossed in four strides, but it was water. When he reached the bank, he glanced up and down, checking for predators.

None. But upstream, where the creek had carved a bank at a curve, the water formed a pool.

Atlatl set his bundle of clothing on the bank and plunged waist-deep into the water. It was so clear, he could see flashes of large fish as they scattered at his movement. Trails of gray formed in the current downstream of Atlatl as the mud slid off his body. He ducked his head in the water and shook the mud clear from his hair. Then he faced upstream, cupped his hands and filled them with water, drinking deeply.

Water had never seemed so good to Atlatl.

Cub crouched on the bank, lapping at the water.

"You need hands!" Atlatl told Cub. "What good are those claws of yours when it comes to drinking?"

Cub saw the fish and made a massive downward swipe with a front paw, splashing water in a geyser.

Another fish and another swipe.

Atlatl saw the silver darts of the fish as they easily avoided Cub's attacks.

"Cub." Atlatl laughed. "That's not how to do it!"

Remembering Clan members fishing in a similar pool during happier times, Atlatl waded back downstream to where the water was shallower. He grabbed a rounded stone high enough that half of it stuck out of the water and moved it to a shallower place. He found a dozen more rocks of similar size and set them into a small circle with a small opening on the upstream side. Water flowed between the rocks, but the gaps were too small for a fish to escape. Now it was a matter of patience and work to guide fish into the trap.

At a slight angle leading away from the opening in the circle, Atlatl set more stones of similar size in a line. He repeated the line on the other side, so that both lines formed a V that fed into the open top of the circle.

By then, Cub had given up on trying to trap fish with his paws and had fallen asleep on the near bank.

Atlatl smiled. Cub was not going to like what Atlatl had in mind.

Atlatl tiptoed up to the animal and patted his head.

Cub opened one eye.

"Time to swim," Atlatl said. He reached under Cub's chest with both arms. Atlatl could barely lift him, Cub had grown so much.

Atlatl straightened, and Cub flailed at the air with all four paws.

Atlatl carried Cub into the center of the pool and dropped him.

Cub squawked and kept flailing. It scattered all the fish downstream toward the end of the pool. Some of them reached the shallow water and tried to escape by wriggling through the V to where it narrowed. Atlatl splashed behind them, scaring them further until the fish swam into the enclosure of rocks that formed a circle.

Cub scrambled onto the bank, shaking water from his fur and glowering at Atlatl.

"Well done, Cub!" Atlatl said.

Four plump fish were trapped, their fins sticking out of the water.

Atlatl grabbed a rock with a sharp edge. When he reached the circle, he smacked the biggest fish on the head and stunned it. Then he reached under the fish's belly and flipped it onto the bank where Cub had retreated.

The fish flopped in a frantic effort to return to water.

Cub pounced. Within seconds, he'd torn the fish apart and gulped down most of it. Cub cocked his head and looked at Atlatl.

"So that's the way it is," Atlatl said. "I do all the work, and you do all the eating?"

Cub growled. For a moment, it seemed as if Cub had answered Atlatl. But Cub's focus had shifted away from the creek to the walls of the gully. His growl deepened and the fur on the back of his neck rose.

Something dangerous was approaching.

Atlatl's tool kit and bundle of clothing were still on the bank. He'd not had time to cut a spear shaft. He had no protection. Naked and without a weapon, he was a slow, clumsy animal with no speed to escape or sharp teeth or claws to protect himself.

He wondered if he had time to try to climb a tree.

Cub's growling became more intense.

Tall bushes halfway down the gully trembled and shook. Whatever predator was behind them, there was no time to get to a tree.

In a crouching walk, Atlatl moved back upstream into the pool. The water would mask his scent and hide most of his body. He doubted that would be enough, but it was all he had.

With his nose just above the water, Atlatl kept his focus on the bushes. He nearly gasped when the massive, dark creature pushed through.

Short-face!

Most types of bears hardly grew bigger than an adult saber-tooth.

Not the short-face. This beast had a skull as wide as a man's chest, with a short snout and small, nearsighted eyes. On all four legs, the short-face had shoulders taller than Atlatl standing on his tiptoes. It was the largest predator that humans ever faced.

Atlatl tried not to breathe as the bear pushed through the bushes and down to the bank of the creek.

Cub growled and backed away.

The bear stood briefly and clawed at the sky, then roared as it dropped down to all fours again.

Cub stood his ground, out of reach of the massive paws that could flip small boulders.

The bear seemed to lose interest in Cub and grunted as if Cub was a minor pest.

Then the bear swung its head in Atlatl's direction.

A small breeze brought Atlatl the rancid smell of the bear's fur. He felt his nostrils flare as he took an involuntary sniff.

He realized, though, that if the breeze was bringing him the bear's scent, it was taking his own scent away from the bear. Short-faces, everyone in the Clan knew, did not have good vision. If Atlatl managed to keep still, perhaps the bear would not realize that the rounded shape sticking out of the water belonged to a human head.

The bear dropped its own head and began to lap at the water.

It seemed to stare directly at Atlatl. It was so close, Atlatl could see the droplets of water on the animal's nose.

Then it stopped lapping and seemed to take closer interest in Atlatl.

Atlatl felt like a giant hand was squeezing his chest.

The bear put one exploratory front paw into the water, then a second paw. It was so close now that Atlatl could have reached out and tapped its nose.

Atlatl kept still. It was his only chance.

Suddenly, there was a splashing sound downstream.

The bear shifted attention away from Atlatl.

The splashing came from the remaining three fish in the stone enclosure in the shallow water.

The short-face grunted. It backed out of the deeper water. It ignored Cub and moved directly to the trapped fish.

The bear plunged a paw into the water and scooped out one of the fish, tossing it onto the bank. It did the same with the second and the third.

Cub darted forward and bit down on one of the fish, then ran far enough down the bank that he was out of reach.

The bear roared and make a short trot toward the remaining fish. It reached down with its jaws and snapped the first fish between its teeth. With a single gulp, the fish disappeared. The second fish followed.

The bear looked around as if wondering where there was more easy food, then grunted again and ambled away from the creek and back into the bushes.

Atlatl closed his eyes in relief.

But his heart sank. He realized that this turn of fortune was only temporary. Without a clan for protection, even the best hunters faced tremendous odds living in solitude. For Atlatl, it would only be a matter of time until a predator like this short-face or a dire wolf or a lion would find him. He wouldn't survive for long.

The best Atlatl could hope for was a chance to confront the Turtle god before he was struck down. Until then, he needed a spear.

Chapter Twenty-One

After the short-face's departure, Atlatl and Cub trapped another half dozen fish. Atlatl decided his leg was too sore to travel farther, and a quick look at the sky told him he had ample time to find a sheltered place to build a fire, which would at least keep predators away during the night.

He gutted the fish easily with his cutting stone and pulled out the backbone and ribs, leaving strips of flesh that would be delicious over the fire. He found a small sapling and cut off a forked branch to cook the fish on.

Atlatl then gathered large pieces of dead wood and arranged them propped against each other on a flat spot where his back was protected by rock face. The rock face would also reflect the heat of the fire during the night.

With the larger pieces of dried wood in place, he found smaller sticks, then twigs. He placed those in the center of the small pile, making sure it wasn't too crowded. Otherwise, not enough air would reach the fuel and the fire would smother.

Finally, he peeled bark from nearby trees and shredded it. This would be the tinder easiest to ignite.

When all was in place, he took out his drilling board from his tool kit. He tied the ends of a leather cord to each end of a stick to use as his bow and placed some shredded bark into a precut hole in the drilling board. He then wound the leather cord twice around a shorter stick. He placed a rock on top of this shorter stick to protect his hands from the heat of friction and placed the other end in the hole with the shredded bark. He sawed back and forth with the bow stick, pushing down with the rock on the shorter stick as it twisted in the hole, creating friction. At the first sign of curling smoke, he blew gently to encourage it to flame, and soon the bark caught fire. He tipped it gently onto the tiny twigs, which soon caught fire, then the smaller branches caught, then the larger pieces of dead wood.

When the fire was hot enough, he placed a strip of raw fish on the forked branch of the sapling and held the fish over the fire. The green wood darkened, but did not catch fire, as the strip of fish began to cook.

Atlatl set the fish aside on a flat rock and cooked a second piece and then a third and fourth. He let the flesh cool and then gorged himself.

He would have been fully content—full and almost sleepy—except now that his basic survival needs had been met, he began to think about the Clan again.

He told himself that perhaps the others had climbed enough to be spared. But the Clan was gone; he knew he was deceiving himself.

Atlatl wanted to sing songs of mourning for each of them.

Did he even have the right? He was no longer part of the Clan. His own father had shunned him. He only had Cub. He felt like he was about to drown in despair. He told himself that if he focused on the tasks of survival, he could swim out of his misery.

So Atlatl stood. He needed a spear shaft.

He sat again. What good would a functional spear do for him? Because of his leg, he'd never be able to throw it with the force needed to kill or protect himself. That left him only the option of being able to hold and jab it in self-defense. Yet a predator like the short-face would push aside a spear as if only a baby were holding it.

If only, Atlatl thought, he could use a throwing stick with a spear the way he did with stones. Except the pouch at the top of his throwing stick would not have held a spear.

He closed his eyes and tried to envision what a throwing stick for a spear might look like. Resting, the spear would need to be secure enough along the top of the throwing stick to not topple off to the side. Yet binding the spear along the top would render it useless. Perhaps a groove the length of the throwing stick would solve that problem.

Atlatl gave it more thought.

Yes! A groove . . .

"Cub!" Atlatl shouted. "I can see it in my mind! A new type of throwing stick for a spear! Stay out of my way!"

Cub, who had been dozing nearby after eating all that fish, didn't even shift, just opened his eyes and closed them again.

Atlatl moved away from the fire, excited to experiment.

He needed one sapling for a spear shaft.

He needed another sapling for the throwing stick, slightly thicker than the spear shaft and about half the length.

He worked hard. Occasionally he had to stop and sharpen his cutting stone. And occasionally he had to drag pieces of dead wood back to the fire to make sure it remained burning.

He didn't even think about how he wasn't thinking about being banished.

As the afternoon disappeared, Cub remained near the fire, doing little but sleeping. Atlatl was astounded to notice that shadows were filling the gully. How had time passed so quickly?

He glanced at the darkening sky. It did not look like it would rain during the night. He simply needed to ensure he had enough fuel to sustain the fire. He set aside the raw saplings he had cut for his spear shaft and throwing stick, and he spent the remaining daylight scouring for more pieces of suitable dead wood. The longer the pieces, the better. During the night, all he'd need to do was push the pieces inward to the fire as the ends burned.

He realized he was hungry again.

With the sky nearly dark, he splashed through the water, trapping more fish.

Then he was ready for an evening at the campfire.

First, he gutted more fish, setting some aside for Cub.

He cooked and ate all the fish, burning the remains so the scent wouldn't bring a predator at night.

Then, with the firelight to give illumination, he turned his attention back to the spear shaft and throwing stick.

Spear shaft first. As he carved away the bark, he made sure to keep the front half of the spear wider and heavier than the rear half. This was the only way to ensure it was balanced as it flew through the air. His time listening on the outskirts of the hunters had taught him that.

When the shaft was smooth and straight, Atlatl cut a notch into the end and held it above the fire to dry and harden it.

He cut some thin strips of leather away from his clothing and soaked them in the creek. He returned to the fire and slid the bottom part of his only spear point into the notch and wrapped the leather around the joint. When the leather dried, it would tighten, keeping the spear point in the notch. It would have been best to have glue from boiled animal hooves, but this would do for now.

Atlatl hefted the spear. It felt balanced enough.

Now the sky was completely dark. He should have been tired and ready for sleep. But his vision of a throwing stick for a spear was too exciting.

He began whittling along the throwing stick. It took patience and steadiness and hours of intense concentration to form a groove from one end of the throwing stick to the other with his burin. As he scraped out chips of wood, he threw them into the fire.

At some point, he laid down to close his eyes and was surprised later to wake up with the light of first dawn at the edge of the horizon. The fire was nearly dead.

Atlatl pushed more of his firewood into the glowing embers and leaned forward and blew on the embers until flames appeared again.

Atlatl reached for his spear. He set the spear shaft atop the groove of the throwing stick. He held the base of the throwing stick in his right hand. The shaft remained balanced on top of the throwing stick.

Atlatl permitted himself a grin of satisfaction.

"I call this a spear thrower," he said to Cub, who was still sleeping off the previous day's exertion. "But it's not quite finished."

He began to scrape the base of the throwing stick to make it narrower at the handle and easier to grip.

By the time dawn had fully arrived, Atlatl was almost ready to begin his journey to confront the Turtle god. He threw all the bark and wood chips into the fire. Atlatl stood and stretched. He scared more fish into the stone enclosure and fed himself and Cub. He trapped and cooked more fish to carry with him and filled his leather bag with water.

Impatient as he was to test the spear thrower, Atlatl reminded himself that his spear point was too precious to risk breaking. He was traveling through land that the Clan had not visited, and there were no certainties he would come across an outcrop of Precious Stone. Until then, his life depended on what remained in his tool kit.

Atlatl gave his cutting stone a critical eye and decided he could sharpen it many times before it was useless.

So he began to cut more spear shafts from saplings. These he did not notch for spear points. Instead, he sharpened the tips and hardened them by heating them in the fire.

Finally, he had an armful of spear shafts, along with his throwing stick and the single spear with a sharp stone point.

He gathered his tools into his kit and pulled the strap over his shoulder.

He gave Cub a quick whistle and climbed out of the gully.

Along the way, he would test his new weapon.

Chapter Twenty-Two

The sky promised more of the same clear, dry weather they had faced the day before. Atlatl was glad he had drunk as deeply as possible from the creek. He touched his water bag to reassure himself that it was not leaking.

In the open grasslands, Atlatl stopped and set down all the sharpened spear shafts in one pile, away from his one stone-tipped spear.

"Cub," Atlatl said. "Let me show you the worst hunter of the Clan."

Atlatl took the first spear shaft and, with only his arm to throw, gave his mightiest heave. The spear wobbled through the air like a duck flying on one wing.

Atlatl grimaced. "See? Old men throw better than that."

He took a second spear. He set it in the groove of his throwing stick. He gripped the narrow base of the throwing stick as if he were holding a spear, his right hand poised to throw. The other end of the throwing stick pointed directly behind him.

Atlatl visualized how he had used the throwing stick to fling rocks. He'd learned that the way to get a rock to go the farthest was to turn his shoulders with his left arm extended in front of him and his right shoulder behind, then turn his body as his right hand came down, bringing the back end of the throwing stick upward and forward.

Atlatl chose a shrub as his target. Atlatl took a breath. He spun his shoulders and replicated that move, imagining the butt end of the throwing stick swinging through at his target.

And the spear just slid off.

"No!" he cried in frustration. He tried it again. Same result each time he tried to throw it. The only way the spear would stay in the groove was if he threw it with such little force that the spear fluttered and landed only a dozen steps away.

Atlatl felt his shoulders droop. All his joy was gone. The idea was useless.

He grabbed one of the spears and started leaning on it to snap it. Why bother carrying tools that were useless?

Just before the spear flexed to the breaking point, Cub growled. A warning growl.

Cub was standing with legs braced, sniffing the breeze, which came from the direction of the gully behind them.

Something threatening was below Atlatl's line of sight. Had the short-face returned? A pack of dire wolves? Lion? Cheetah? More than likely, he thought, it was the short-face. Atlatl had thrown all of the fish remains into the fire again that morning to keep scent from enticing the animal, but perhaps it was hoping to find more fish trapped in the stone enclosure of the creek.

Atlatl was downwind, so he left his practice spears behind to creep back toward the gully to find out what was spooking Cub. There was a point where the path doubled back on itself, and it gave him a view of the creek. He snuck downward and then slowly crawled to a shrub he could peek through to get a view of what was below.

What he saw astounded him.

The predator was another human.

Nootau.

His father was in the pool where the bank curved, washing dried mud off his skin.

Atlatl blinked as he tried to understand what this meant.

Nootau had followed him to the creek. For a skilled hunter, tracking animals came as naturally as breathing, and Atlatl would have been easy to track, being the only other human around.

But Nootau was just now bathing himself of the dried mud from his climb out of the valley. Had he stayed behind a full day before beginning to track Atlatl? Or had he been spying on Atlatl since the day before and been forced to wait for Atlatl to leave before cleaning the mud off himself?

Either way, the bigger question was *why*. What was his father trying to accomplish?

Atlatl could not think of an answer.

He did know, however, that Nootau could have caught up if he'd wanted. Which meant he didn't want to—he was continuing to shun Atlatl.

So Atlatl backed away from the shrub. He drew upon his resolve and anger yet again to force himself to leave his father behind. He moved back up the path to the top of the gully and picked up the practice spears.

If his father was following him, Atlatl refused to leave behind the childlike spears to give Nootau yet another reason to belittle him.

At the campfire that evening, with a couple of hours of daylight remaining, Atlatl ate some of the cooked fish he had carried since morning, sharing the remainder with Cub.

To the side was the last of the practice spears he'd carried all day. The others he'd already burned, and this one was next.

On the ground, too, was his tool kit. One by one, he pulled out the contents, wondering what he could use from it to find food once the fish was gone.

Atlatl surveyed the possessions that had once given him pride when he had foolishly believed he could someday become a hunter. Now, they were just a reminder that while his hands could use the tools to form weapons, his body would never have the strength needed to hurl a spear.

Along with his hammerstone, cutting rock and drilling board, he had an awl, which he used to shred plant fibers. He also had some long slivers of bone that made excellent needles. On the widened end of each of these, he'd used the awl to punch eye holes to hold thread made from grass or thinly sliced strips of leather.

He had a scraper, so sharp on the sides that careless use could tear through the flesh of a finger. And he had a pouch of red ochre.

He began to put his tools back in their leather bag, but realized there was one last tool inside that he'd forgotten to examine.

He pulled it loose. It was his burin, the carving tool he'd used to make the useless grooves down the center of the spear thrower.

Atlatl snorted with disgust, seeing in his mind the practice spears slide out of the groove each time he'd attempted to throw it earlier. What good did gentle throws do if that's what it took for the spear to stay in the groove long enough to fly forward.

A thought struck him.

If the spear was sliding out when force was being applied, didn't that mean the thrower *was* adding force? The spear just needed to stay in the groove—perhaps the thrower wasn't a total failure!

He found himself looking closer at the beak-shaped top of his burin. If he could make a knob like that at the back of the spear thrower to hold the butt of the spear in place throughout the throw . . .

Atlatl was awake before dawn, trying to tamp down his excitement to try the new spear thrower that he'd carved. The evening before, there had been enough daylight to find a new branch to cut as a spear thrower, this one with a knob in place from natural growth.

Like the previous night, he'd spent hours in the dark at the light of the fire carving a groove down the center, and when he'd been able to slide a spear in the groove and push the end of it against the knob, he'd finally allowed himself to sleep.

"Cub," he said. "Look at that shrub ahead of us. Is that about the size of a deer?"

Cub didn't answer.

Atlatl prepared himself for disappointment.

He stood and placed his last remaining practice spear in the groove. With his hand above his right shoulder, he held the bottom end of the spear thrower. In one quick motion, he pulled his hand down and forward, as if throwing a stone.

He watched in disbelief as the spear shaft whistled through the air, going four times the distance of his normal spear throw. The spear went badly wide of the shrub; his accuracy was not impressive at all. But the force of the throw had been amazing.

"Cub! Did you see that?!"

Cub yawned.

"You're just jealous because all you have are claws," Atlatl said, as he went to fetch the spear. "I'll give you another chance to behold how I have just become the mightiest hunter of the Clan."

The Clan. Atlatl closed his eyes in sorrow. He stood motionless for long moments, remembering happier times with his people. Telling stories, sitting at the fire, huddled together in tipis, picking berries, weaving ropes, singing songs.

When he felt the first sting of tears, he opened his eyes and blinked them away. No longer would he permit himself the luxury of weeping. Being part of the Clan was now a part of his past, he told himself, not a part of his future. There was no going back to the past. His father had shunned him. If they had survived, Powaw and Takhi were now together. The rest of the Clan was dead. Except for Cub, Atlatl was alone. He would remain that way for the rest of his life—long life or short life, and more than likely short.

To ensure his life was as long as possible, then, he needed to be able to use a spear as well as any of the hunters of the Clan.

Atlatl opened his eyes and picked up the practice spear. Again, he balanced it on the groove on top of the throwing stick, and again, he made sure the butt of the spear was solidly in place against the branch nub at the back of the throwing stick. He tried keeping his forearm straight to get better accuracy.

He hit the side of the shrub. Not perfect, but better.

"Cub!" At least he had someone to share his joy with, someone who wouldn't judge him or scorn him.

He walked to the shrub to retrieve his spear. It was a satisfyingly long walk. It gave him an idea to help pass the time.

As he traveled to the land of ice, he flung the spear ahead of him, watching with a grin as it sailed far, far ahead. This is what he would do. Walk, throw, retrieve. Teaching himself to use his new weapon.

Chapter Twenty-Three

Atlatl heard the trumpeting of the mammoths before seeing them.

Three days of uneventful walking had taken Atlatl and Cub from hills with clusters of trees to undulating grasslands with occasional clumps of shrubs. Berries and cooked fish and water from occasional streams sustained them.

Atlatl would look back occasionally, but he saw no sign of Nootau. His father would have had no difficulty tracking him. At the least, the fires that Atlatl built each night would have served as a beacon easily visible from a long distance away. But Nootau—if he was still following—was keeping his distance.

As Atlatl had reached the top of each new hill, he'd been able to see the dark purple line on the horizon that marked the mountains of the north where he expected to find Ghost Mountain and the land of the gods.

Atlatl had been working his way up another hill when the distinctive sound of the mammoths alerted him to their presence on the other side. Atlatl was curious about the size of the herd and made his way to the top. Below, gathered near a small lake, was a group of adults and juveniles.

Most of the herd was at rest, their tails in constant motion swatting insects. A couple of males were engaging in a playful pushing contest, and they were the ones whose trumpeting had caught Atlatl's attention.

Although Atlatl had thrown his practice spear hundreds of times and thought he'd be able to hurl his spear with enough speed to pierce a mammoth hide, he knew better than to attempt it.

Mammoths were extremely intelligent. Much as dire wolves coordinated their efforts to hunt in packs, mammoths in herds were formidable opponents. The Clan would hunt only juveniles or injured or ill adults, and then only with a group of hunters.

If Atlatl threw a spear as a single hunter, the mammoths as a group would stampede toward him in fury. He'd be unable to outrun them, so he certainly had no chance of escape.

Cub showed no interest in the mammoths. Atlatl stayed on the crest of the hill to circle around the herd and continued north, practicing spear throws along the way.

Toward the end of the day, Atlatl saw an animal worth pursuing.

Long-nose pig!

There were two types of pigs that the Clan hunted. The short-nose pigs tended to live in herds and often gathered in caves. Like the mammoths, they would turn on a hunter as a group. But the long-nose preferred to root around trees and bushes alone.

Near a protective clump of thorny bushes, a long-nose below was pawing at the ground with a front hoof. Whatever it was trying to dig drew its full attention. There was a favorable wind, blowing from the long-nose toward Atlatl.

More movement.

Atlatl grinned. This was a mother, with two young ones.

The mother was about the size of Cub. Each of the young ones looked well past the weaning stage. The mother was dangerous, with tusks that could rip open a belly. But if Atlatl could spear one of the small ones, the food could sustain him for days.

Atlatl slid his stone-point spear into the groove of his spear thrower. Arm poised, he slowly moved forward, hoping for stealth. He was so intent on the hunt, he didn't notice that Cub had disappeared.

He was almost within throwing distance when Cub leaped from the tall grass, paws coming down on the hind end of one of the small pigs. It bolted, and Cub's claws only succeeded in raking its hind end. The pig squealed and twisted, dodging Cub's efforts to sink his long dagger teeth into its belly.

At the same time, the second twin bolted with a squeal of its own, headed directly toward Atlatl.

This was his moment to test the spear. But a moving object was too difficult to hit.

Atlatl shouted at the pig, and the sudden sound shocked it into stopping. It was about twenty paces away, a perfect distance for Atlatl's spear thrower.

Atlatl tensed his shoulder muscles, ready to throw.

In that moment, the pig disappeared in a flash of black. It was so unexpected that Atlatl couldn't understand what had happened until the flash of black became the shape of huge wings flapping.

The thunderbird had swooped in, claws extended. Now the pig kicked as it dangled below the thunderbird's massive body. The bird strained to lift the weight of the animal, and for a long moment, appeared motionless as those massive wings flapped. The tips of its wings slapped the ground, raising dust.

To kill the thunderbird, all that Atlatl needed to do was rotate his shoulders and fling his spear. He knew at this distance there was no way he'd miss a target of this size.

Yet he lowered his arm.

If the thunderbird had been forced to flee the valley because of the flood, Atlatl would not kill it. It would be meaningless to decorate himself with a necklace holding the bird's beak and claws if Atlatl had no Clan to see his trophy. Besides which, he felt a connection to this incredible animal.

Beyond the thunderbird, Cub was still chasing the other young pig. Both animals zigzagged, kicking up dust.

The thunderbird gained height, still holding its prey. The pig screeched in terror as the monstrous bird of prey rose to the sky.

Atlatl heard a different squeal. This one was of rage.

The mother pig was in a direct dash at Atlatl, armed with tusks that could disembowel a human.

No time to think.

With a single smooth motion, Atlatl rotated his shoulders and flung his arm forward, aiming his hand at the enraged sow as if he were throwing a rock. The spear sizzled with speed, and with a solid thump an instant later, it pierced the chest of the long-nose.

She plowed forward a few steps, faltered, then toppled.

"Ei-yee!" Atlatl shouted. "Ei-yee!"

So this was the triumph of a successful hunter!

His yelling drew Cub's attention. By then, the other young pig had escaped into the bush.

Atlatl moved to where the thunderbird had swooped down.

In the dust, he saw markings where the huge bird's wing tips had slapped the ground.

With reverence, he paced it off. Four full strides from one tip to the other. The bird's wingspread was almost as wide as a short-face bear standing on its hind legs was tall.

Atlatl remembered the story he'd told the children of the Clan. How a thunderbird had knocked him over the edge of a cliff and how he'd bravely fought for his life and forced the thunderbird to leave him alone.

Atlatl remembered, too, that all of the older members of the Clan would give him amused smiles of tolerance as he told the story. Nobody really believed it, except for him.

And no wonder. Thunderbirds were so rare that, in a lifetime, a human might see it only once or twice. And no child could survive a bird of prey this big. Atlatl had been such a good storyteller, he'd convinced himself that the thunderbird story was true.

It plainly could not be truth at all. No child would have been able to fend off a bird this monstrous.

No wonder his own father could not hide his scorn at Atlatl.

To the side of the markings in the sand was a purple-black pinion feather that must have come loose from the thunderbird's wing. It was easily twice as big as a feather from any other bird in the Clan's existence.

Atlatl would keep it. Not to help him remember this afternoon with the thunderbird. Instead, as a reminder that if he ever found a Clan again, he would tell stories only to share truths and memories, not to try and impress others.

He wove some of his hair around the quill of the feather and let the feather hang behind his shoulder as decoration.

Then he pulled his cutting stone out of his tool kit. He and Cub were about to enjoy a feast.

Chapter Twenty-Four

Since last sighting Nootau, Atlatl had traveled in a meandering line toward the land of ice, never straying far from the top of the hills that led back down into the Valley of the Turtle.

As they walked, he told Cub a story about each of the members of the Clan. Every time he told a story, the person seemed alive to him again. Every time he told a story, his anger grew at the Turtle god for sending a flood to destroy the Clan, and as his anger grew, so did his resolve to confront the Turtle god in their honor.

On occasion, he'd wandered to his left—the direction of the setting sun—to look down into the valley and marvel at the damage left behind by the Great Flood. Every time he had made a trip to overlook the path of the flood, he saw that nothing remained below except mud and rock as far as he could see up and down the valley, with a small ribbon of water to mark the path of the river.

He could measure progress by how the valley narrowed the farther he walked. The hills on each side were steeper too. Here, the water must have been flowing much faster, compressed by the chute walls. In places, trunks of torn trees were scattered above the top of the valley, evidence that there had been so much water it had spilled over.

Except for the increasing cold under clouded skies, progress was not difficult. The terrain had transitioned completely from trees to grasslands to rocky tundra with red lichens. Infrequent patches of snow and ice began to cover more and more of the tundra, and the only animals he spotted were hares and foxes that kept a safe distance from him and Cub.

Streams and shallow rivers of icy water cut lines through the treeless expanse, all flowing toward the Valley of the Turtle, most of them easy enough to cross. Where they were too wide and too deep and too fast moving, Atlatl simply followed them upstream far enough to find a place to safely ford.

As his journey continued, what caught Atlatl's attention most was the low line of gray that, at a distance, had seemed to stretch across the horizon. After days and days of travel, the band of dark gray now seemed swirling and alive.

Atlatl and Cub reached the top of a gently rising hill, and for the first time, Atlatl was close enough to see that up ahead, sheer white cliffs rose to disappear into the gray band of cloud.

Ghost Mountain.

He stopped so quickly that Cub bumped into his leg.

"It is just as the hunters have described it," Atlatl whispered to Cub, as if he were close enough that the gods might be able to hear him. "Behind it must be the great lake where the Turtle god lives."

Despite his resolution not to let memories of his past weaken him, Atlatl closed his eyes and began to sing a song of mourning. He felt like his grandmother's spirit was beside him as a guide.

Atlatl eased himself into a sitting position, mesmerized by the sight of the white cliffs. The mountain was monstrous in size, bigger and more imposing than Atlatl could have imagined. The Turtle god suddenly seemed much more real to him. "If Turtle was mighty enough to send such a flood . . ."

Atlatl didn't finish his thoughts out loud.

How foolish he had been. He had allowed anger and petulance to make him think he was brave enough to confront a god. But that was when the concept of a god was just that: a concept.

Atlatl drew up his knees and hugged his legs, staring at the ice cliffs ahead, imagining what it might be to confront the Turtle god.

Did gods even speak as humans spoke?

And if Atlatl were to shake a fist in fury at this god for destroying the Clan, would this god respond?

All he needed was a memory of the massive short-face bear to remind him how fragile a human was without a clan. How much more terrifying than a bear was a god capable of sending such a flood?

Would a god strike him dead for daring to question the action of the gods?

Even with his shivers of fear, Atlatl could feel his anger rising again.

"Wawetseka," Atlatl said aloud. "You once walked the earth. You sang. You taught. You comforted. Turtle destroyed you."

Atlatl hummed a high keening sound in mourning for Wawetseka.

"Kiwi," Atlatl said. "You once walked the earth. You sang. You laughed. Turtle destroyed you."

He hummed his mourning sound again.

"Nuna," Atlatl said. "You once walked the earth. You sang. You danced. Turtle destroyed you."

He felt tears as he mourned each one of the Clan.

His anger and resolve had returned. He would face Turtle and honor the memories of the Clan.

He reached into his tool kit and found his pouch of red ochre. He sang more songs of mourning and painted his face.

Then he continued his journey to Ghost Mountain.

Atlatl remembered what hunters said about Ghost Mountain: a world of ice from where the sun rises to where it sets, to the ends of the world beyond.

Seeing it now, Atlatl understood. At the head of the valley, the snowy wall of Ghost Mountain did extend from one side to the other as far as he could see. He imagined the edge of the ice extending ahead of him too, far into the distance. Nothing could live in that land of ice. Except, perhaps, the gods who did not want humans to intrude on their lives.

From his vantage point at the top of the valley hills, Atlatl saw that along the wall, protruding like a huge tongue, was a slope of more ice licking downward, with monstrous ice blocks that had broken loose from the wall and tumbled to the base. Along the top of the tongue were parallel bands of rock and gravel, as if the giant walls of ice behind it were spitting out debris. Water seeped from under the base, forming serpent streams of various sizes that carved through deposits of gravel.

Atlatl couldn't see what was behind this tongue of ice, but the floodwaters seemed to have come from there. This, then, was where he needed to go to find where the flood started. He began to descend into the valley.

When he reached the bottomlands, the leathers of his foot skins were soaked completely, and the water was near the temperature of freezing. Atlatl shivered. Without his skin clothing, it would have been impossible.

When Atlatl reached yet another shallow stream flowing away from the ice mountain, he sucked in a breath at the sight of a huge paw print. It was part of a set of tracks leading away from the mountain, to the south.

A short-face?

He looked in all directions and saw no movement.

When he shivered now, it wasn't from the cold. Atlatl could easily fit both of his own feet, front to back, inside the center of one of the tracks. The imprint was so distinct, he could see the furrows of claws. He knelt and placed his hand along the ground. Each claw mark was as long as his hand.

He watched Cub carefully. Cub did not react to the smell of the tracks. With no dirt to blow across this frozen land, the prints could have been made days earlier.

To drive away his fear, Atlatl decided he should have a conversation with Cub.

For Cub's benefit, Atlatl pointed upward at the heights of Ghost Mountain. "There is no way to climb. And no purpose. What god would live atop of that?"

Cub didn't answer.

"That's where the water is coming from, and that's where Turtle will be," Atlatl told Cub, pointing to the tip of the ice tongue. "I've come this far. Bear tracks or not, I'm not going to stop now. I'll understand if you stay here and wait."

Cub followed.

➤

Atlatl could not see the sun because of the cloud above the ice, but when he sensed it was midday, they reached where the ice tongue came out of the mountain. While it was shorter than the walls of Ghost Mountain, the ice tongue was still much taller than the largest of trees. They would now have to veer in a downstream direction and around the tongue to see what was on the other side.

When he reached the bottom of the ice tongue and began to round the corner, Atlatl felt a change in the breeze for the first time since beginning their trek. It had been coming from the land of ice, off the mountain, but without warning, now it was in his face.

"Storm?" Atlatl asked Cub, looking upward to see if the clouds had changed as well. With the breeze came a low moaning sound.

All Atlatl could see was ice to the right, and gravel and hummocks to the left. The view would open ahead, where the edge of the ice tongue curved back to the north.

"Perhaps the gods do wait for us," Atlatl told Cub, his voice grim. The moaning sound made him shiver with fear.

Atlatl let out a deep breath. He scratched the top of Cub's head and took comfort in their friendship.

He took a step, then paused. Had he heard a voice above the moaning sound ahead of him?

"Atlatl!"

Were the gods calling out to him?

Atlatl turned toward the sound and saw, at a far distance behind him along the edge of the ice tongue, his father.

"Atlatl!"

Nootau was waving with frantic motions.

Atlatl waved back, puzzled. Why, after all this time following him, had his father now decided to reveal himself?

"Atlatl!" Nootau began to dash toward Atlatl, pointing with jabs of his spear. The wind had been blowing away from the mountain and from Atlatl. And from where it came, the predator tracking Atlatl's scent: moving toward him at a shuffling half-run was the short-face.

Chapter Twenty-Five

Atlatl was certain to die.

A group of three or more hunters might safely kill a short-face, standing apart at different angles to throw spears from the safety of a ledge or a tree.

But Atlatl was not highly skilled. Nootau was too far away to make it to his side so they could stand together against the bear. There were no trees to climb. The walls of the ice tongue were too sheer to be able to get a handhold. And he couldn't outrun a short-face.

The bear loomed as it ran in a straight line toward Atlatl. Atlatl's only chance was his spear thrower. Even so, it would take astounding luck to pierce a vital organ deep enough to kill the short-face before it charged the final distance between them.

With his hands almost numb from cold, Atlatl managed to set his spear on the groove of the spear thrower. He lifted his arm, ready to strike, and prepared for his death. Beside him, Cub growled and squared himself to the approaching animal.

Saliva flew from the bear's muzzle as it galloped toward him.

Nootau screamed. The short-face slowed and paused.

Nootau screamed again and began to run toward the bear, continuing to scream.

Running *toward* the short-face.

Atlatl blinked, puzzled again.

The short-face tilted its massive head in Nootau's direction, assessing the threat.

Atlatl heard the bear grunt. It shifted direction and started galloping toward Nootau.

Nootau immediately stopped.

"Atlatl, run! Run! Find safety!" Nootau began to back away, the fearsome monster in full pursuit.

There was no way his father could take on the short-face alone.

He was sacrificing himself for Atlatl.

"Run!" Nootau shouted.

The bear roared and closed the distance on Nootau. Gravel clattered as its paws slammed the ground.

Atlatl pushed off as hard as he could from his good leg, and with great limping strides, tried to cover ground as quickly as possible. Not away from the bear. But to his father.

"Ei-yee!" Atlatl shouted the hunter's cry. "Ei-yee!"

But it was also a cry of despair. He wouldn't get there in time.

"Ei-yee!" Atlatl shouted. Maybe more noise would distract the short-face again. "Ei-yee!"

The short-face slowed, almost to a complete stop, halfway between Atlatl and Nootau. It swung its head back and forth, its skull almost as big as a small pig, trying to choose which prey to attack.

"As your father, I command you to run!" Nootau yelled past the short-face to Atlatl. "You still have a chance."

"We each move toward it," Atlatl called back. His spear thrower was poised. His father was too far away to hurl a spear with any hope of piercing the short-face's hide, but by now, after all his practice throws, Atlatl knew he was in range. "We keep it in the middle. I throw first. Then you run in and throw from your side. It's our only chance."

"No!" Nootau shouted. "You are too far away. It won't work!"

In confused anger, the bear stood on its hind legs and

bellowed. For Atlatl, the beast seemed to fill the sky. With the bear's belly exposed, Atlatl had the perfect chance to make a killing throw.

Atlatl reared on his back leg and started to rotate his shoulders for a mighty throw.

But his foot slipped on the frozen gravel, and he fell sideways onto his bad leg. His spear clattered off the groove of his spear thrower.

Ribs bruised from impact on the frozen ground, Atlatl tried scrambling backward as the bear dropped onto all fours and spun and charged Atlatl. Each stride took it farther out of range from Nootau's spear.

Then a blur of brown-orange fur leaped over Atlatl's shoulder to charge at the short-face.

Cub!

Atlatl had never heard such rage from Cub. The screeching roar was so loud that the short-face skidded in hesitation. Cub launched, paws and claws extended. The short-face twisted and raised a front leg in defense.

Atlatl didn't see what happened next. He was on his feet again, grabbing the spear that had fallen nearby. He felt no numbness in his hands, just a terrible calm as he slid the spear onto the groove of the thrower and set his sights on the bear.

Cub had buried his front fangs in the shoulders of the short-face. The bear shook side to side and Cub slipped to the ground. With a monstrous swipe of a front paw, the short-face flung Cub almost to Atlatl's feet.

The bear turned to Atlatl, opening its jaws wide and roaring with a shake of its head.

Time seemed to freeze. Sound disappeared. Atlatl felt no sensation.

His concentration was so focused and his vision was so sharp that the individual hairs on the short-face's shoulders were etched against the gray sky. He brought his hand forward and released the spear in a fluid straight line.

Sound returned. The whiz of the spear. The thud as the spear point flew into the short-face's open mouth, driving into the back of its throat.

With a terrible gurgling, the short-face clawed uselessly at the shaft, losing balance and toppling sideways.

Atlatl felt a bloodlust beyond anything he'd experienced before, a tingling rush of blood that seemed to expand his skin and muscles.

"Ei-yee!" Atlatl screamed. For a moment, he was beyond rational thought. "Ei-yee!"

His hand was in his tool kit and, without knowing how he got there, he was standing over the short-face with only hands and cutting stone, ready to leap on the bear's giant body.

"Ei-yee!" he screamed again. "Ei-yee!"

The sound of his name brought him back.

He blinked. The short-face was motionless.

"Atlatl! Atlatl!" Nootau was there, pushing him away from the fallen short-face. "Atlatl!"

Atlatl felt himself breathing again, heaving for air.

He fell to his knees.

Nootau knelt beside him. Nootau's voice lost urgency and was filled with wonder instead.

"Atlatl . . . ," Nootau whispered. "Had I not seen this, I would not have believed it possible."

Nootau stood again and paced from front to back along the body of the short-face. Five full paces.

Nootau needed both hands to lift one of the paws. He held it in front of him, astonished. The paw covered his entire chest.

By then, Atlatl was standing too.

Nootau leaned over the top of the bear. He shook his head in renewed disbelief and touched the back of the bear's neck. "The spear point. Look."

Atlatl limped beside his father. The point of the stone had gone completely through the hide and was sticking out the back of the animal's neck.

"This . . ." Nootau could not find words. "You . . ."

A whimper of pain pulled Atlatl's attention away from the body of the short-face.

Cub.

Atlatl hobbled over to Cub as Cub was trying to crawl forward. Cub's back legs weren't moving. Blood streamed from his mouth.

"Cub," Atlatl said softly.

Atlatl was afraid that lifting Cub would hurt him, so he sat beside him instead. Cub crawled onto his lap and laid his head on Atlatl's thighs.

"Cub," Atlatl whispered again. "Cub."

Atlatl leaned forward to cradle Cub's chest. Cub's gasps for air became weaker and weaker. Nootau sat beside Atlatl and wordlessly put an arm around Atlatl's shoulder as Cub left the land of the living.

Chapter Twenty-Six

When Atlatl finally lifted his head to look at his father, Nootau's eyes were shiny with tears.

Tears?

"Nootau, I—"

"Not another word!" Nootau's face was contorted with the emotion that choked his voice.

Nootau leaned over and hugged Atlatl so ferociously that Atlatl could hardly breathe. His father had never hugged him before. It was a wonderful sensation, so strangely mixed with Atlatl's sorrow to be holding Cub's lifeless body.

Finally, Nootau pushed away and held Atlatl at arm's length and studied Atlatl as if he had never seen him before.

"As I followed you," Nootau said, "I crept close to your fire at night. I listened to you tell stories to this loyal beast that refused to leave your side. So many times I wanted to call out to you and tell you that I was sorry. That it was wrong to drive you away because I was angry at what happened to the Clan. Yet I was too proud. I am sorry for that too. And then, to think that I might have lost you to a short-face . . ."

Nootau gave a half sob.

Sorry? Atlatl had never heard his father apologize to anyone for anything.

"You look much like a man I know named Nootau," Atlatl said. "Are you a spirit living inside his body?"

Atlatl heard from his father another sound that was unfamiliar. Laughter.

Nootau cuffed him affectionately across the head. "Listen, my son. I've watched you all these days. You are as man as anyone I've ever known. But you might not want to push me too far."

Nootau glanced at the sky. "The night will be on us too soon. We will need a fire. There is very little wood here. Downstream—"

"No," Atlatl said. "Not downstream. Not yet."

Nootau frowned. "There is nothing in any other direction except ice."

"On the other side of this ice tongue is the Turtle

god," Atlatl said. "Where the river flows out of the ice wall."

"The Turtle god?" Nootau's frown deepened.

"After you shunned me . . . ," Atlatl said. He was very conscious of Cub's body in his lap. Yet his father so rarely spoke, it seemed like if he didn't ask now, he might never get the chance again. "Why did you follow me?"

Nootau took a few steps away and, with his back to Atlatl, stared at the dead short-face. When he turned around again, there was a sad smile on his face.

"At first, regret," Nootau said, kneeling so his face was level with Atlatl's face. "Even as I shunned you with my silence, I knew I was wrong. It's not because of you that the Great Flood happened. I just wanted someone to blame."

Atlatl kept his chin steady.

"That regret became something else as I watched you on the mud bank, sliding down again and again, yet somehow climbing a little higher each time until you reached the top of the hill and marched away without looking back. I realized it didn't matter to me that you couldn't hunt or that your leg is shattered. You're my son. You've always made people like you with stories and by making them laugh. Or playing tricks.

Like Banti. I didn't appreciate it. But he doesn't have what I saw in you. Something strong inside. A fierceness I did not know was there. Determination. These are your gifts, and they are just as vital to the Clan as any hunter."

Nootau ruefully shook his head. "Then I became curious. You seemed to have a destination in mind. So I stayed with you, trusting that during the day you would manage to survive. And at night, well, I was close enough to protect you. But you didn't need it. And now you tell me that your destination is a search for the Turtle god?"

"The Turtle god destroyed the Clan."

"You intend to punish the Turtle god?" Nootau snorted. "The gods . . ."

Nootau tilted his head, as if thinking about this for the first time. Then he set his jaw, his conclusion firm. "The gods created our world. They don't live among us."

"I do not intend to punish the Turtle god," Atlatl said. "I want to ask why the Turtle god chose to destroy our family."

Nootau shook his head. "That is not for us to ask."

"I will ask." Atlatl pointed away from them, toward the place where he'd heard the strange moaning and where the wind had shifted into his face. "If the flood was because of a god, he will hear my stories."

"You and your stories."

"If the Turtle god sent the flood and destroyed the Clan, the Turtle god will listen to me sing songs of mourning to honor every member of the Clan."

"No," Nootau said. "Humans do not visit the gods."

"Then I go alone."

Atlatl watched his father's face darken.

"You travel with me," Nootau said. "We follow the valley back to our lands. First, we take what we need from this short-face. The claws are yours, for a necklace like none other in the history of the Clan."

Before Atlatl could disagree again, Nootau shook his head and pointed at Atlatl's spear thrower. "How was it done?"

Wordlessly, Atlatl handed Nootau the spear thrower.

When it was in Nootau's hands, he turned it over and over again, examining every detail.

With reverence, Nootau placed the spear thrower back into Atlatl's hands.

"You will help me carve one of my own," Nootau said. Not a demand, but the request of one man to another. "And you will teach me how to throw it like it is part of my own hand."

"In return," Atlatl said, "after we take what we can from the short-face, you will accompany me to the Turtle god."

Nootau finally nodded. "We have something far more important to do first."

Nootau placed a hand softly on Cub's head and closed the animal's eyes. "I would be honored to help you sing a song of mourning for Cub."

Atlatl took the pouch with red ochre out of his tool kit and reached out to paint his father's face.

Chapter Twenty-Seven

Skinning the short-face took much of the afternoon. The ceremony to send Cub to the land of the ancestors took the evening. The night was cold, and there was no wood or mammoth bones to burn on the tundra, but Atlatl and Nootau were able to huddle under the uncured hide of the short-face, turning the fur toward them. Neither spoke during the night. For Atlatl, there was contentment in knowing that his father accepted him.

In the morning, Nootau folded the fur, determined to carry it back south with them. Atlatl's only burdens were the enormous bear claws for his necklace and the sorrow of remembering how Cub had saved his life.

When they were finally ready to leave the carcass of the short-face, Nootau said, "I don't like this, continuing onward to face the Turtle god. But I have made my bargain with you."

"I want to at least see where the Great Flood began," Atlatl said. "If the Turtle god is nowhere to be seen, I will turn around."

When they reached the tip of the ice tongue, Atlatl again felt that change in the breeze.

"Storm?" Nootau asked, echoing Atlatl's question the day before. He paused and looked upward to see if the clouds had changed as well.

"It was the same when I reached here before," Atlatl said. "As was the sound."

Nootau frowned at the low moaning that came from ahead of them.

"It is like nothing I have experienced before," Nootau said, his voice grim. "Perhaps the gods do wait for us around the bend."

Atlatl said, "It should open up ahead of us, and we will see what is there. And then we will know."

Nootau gave a grunt of discontent but began to walk again.

Atlatl followed and they came around the downstream tip of the ice tongue. The view to the north opened in front of them.

Atlatl gasped.

Here, abruptly, neither the ice tongue nor Ghost Mountain existed in front of them. Nor did the flat graveled land of hummocks and shallow streams. The moaning came from the wind that howled through a chasm in the solid ice wall of Ghost Mountain, a chasm that formed a sheer-walled canyon so wide and deep that it would have taken half a day to walk across. The canyon floor was rock and mud where the Great Flood had torn through it, with a fast slashing river still cutting down the middle. As for the ice mountain, it was like a monstrous fist had punched straight through it, shattering it all the way up to the line of clouds.

The huge gap in the ice was a staggering sight. Ghost Mountain was a massively thick wall of ice: had they been able to walk through the gap into the moaning wind, it would have also taken a half day to reach the other side.

For long, long moments, neither Atlatl nor Nootau spoke as they tried to comprehend a world beyond imagination.

"The story is true, then," Nootau said, his voice a whisper of awe. "The Turtle god was bound and thrown into a lake so deep that he should never have escaped. See, that's how high the water was."

Nootau pointed through the gap to the other side of the mountain. Showing how high the water had once been, almost to the top of the overhanging clouds, was a line that separated dark mud from undisturbed tundra.

Atlatl stared at the chasm, trying to picture a turtle large enough to cause such damage. Then, suddenly, he understood. This section of Ghost Mountain had been acting as a dam, holding back an expanse of water far, far deeper than any lake in the lands to the south, so immense that, when it released, it had filled the entire Valley of the Turtle all the days and days of travel downstream. Even now, at the bottom of the canyon, water still poured through in a fast-moving river.

"Will you still demand that the Turtle god hear your mourning songs?" Nootau asked. "To any god big enough to smash through this ice mountain, we would be like ants beneath the foot of a mammoth."

"There is no Turtle god," Atlatl answered.

"Only something as mighty as a god could do this," his father said. "Something beyond our understanding."

"Then it was a hungry god of water." Atlatl looked back at the ice tongue and the streams of water that ran through the gravel from the base of it.

"Hungry?" Nootau said.

"Water eats the ice." Atlatl knew he was right. Before the flood, over days and days and days, the river in the Valley of the Turtle had been rising and rising as the water ate away at the bottom of the ice mountain. This water had been slowly making the river rise until the ice had finally weakened enough for the water to punch through the dam.

Nootau gave his own nod of comprehension. "The water god."

Perhaps, Atlatl thought, the ice would grow back. And the lake would fill behind it again. And someday, when enough time passed, there would be too much water and it would eat the ice again.

In another flash, Atlatl understood something much more important. If it could happen in the future, it could have happened in the past.

"The Turtle god," Atlatl said. "The Elders gave us the story of Turtle to protect us. We were meant to pass it down to others. It doesn't matter if you believe in the Turtle god—it's the story that matters."

Atlatl understood what Wawetseka had been trying to tell him. That was the power of story: it let people believe without seeing things for themselves. Truth was in what a story meant.

"We did not listen," Nootau said. He was quiet for a long time. "No. I did not listen. I did not move the Clan when the marker stone told us of the danger. The Clan is gone because of me."

Nootau put his hands on Atlatl's shoulders. "Are you hearing what I say? It is not the Turtle god you need to confront with your stories. It is me. This was never your fault. We must face all of those at the Gathering so that I can accept my punishment there."

Part Three

THE GATHERING

Chapter Twenty-Eight

"Smoke!" Atlatl said, looking down the valley from their viewpoint high in the hills. Nootau preferred staying at elevations that gave them as much overview of the landscape as possible. It was easier to see predators at a distance, and for the same reason, easier to see prey. Also, the more land that their eyes could sweep, the easier it was to navigate and the easier it would be to spot the Gathering.

At each bend of the meandering river below, Atlatl had scanned as far ahead as possible, hoping to see any sign that the Gathering of Clans had not dispersed.

Six days of uneventful travel had taken them this far, with Nootau unerringly guiding them based on landmarks indistinguishable to the untrained eye. Because they weren't carrying bundles of skin and sticks for tents, Atlatl and Nootau had moved swiftly, even with the burden of the short-face pelt. In the evenings, Atlatl had patiently drilled holes in the bear's front claws until all ten were ready for him to string around his neck. During those same hours of relaxation, Nootau carved a spear thrower and began to practice with it.

It had been six days filled with companionable silences.

Nootau seemed a changed man. Not so arrogant and demanding. He still said little, and Atlatl was okay with that. He no longer needed to hear his father's every thought in order to feel loved and accepted. Nootau, however, had encouraged Atlatl to tell stories, and seemed to enjoy them. During their silences, Atlatl had spent most of his walking hours remembering moments with Cub, remembering stories about the Clan.

Soon, finally, he'd find out if Takhi and Powaw had survived and found the Gathering. Thinking about what was ahead gave him a strange mixture of antici-pation and dread. Mixed in with those emotions was pride. Ten massive claws from the short-face bear hung on leather lace in a necklace that bumped on his chest. While everyone in all the clans would see his unmistak-able limp with each step he took, everyone in all the clans would also see those claws and know that Atlatl and his spear thrower had conquered a short-face.

If Takhi was alive, she, too, could take pride in that.

"Smoke," Nootau agreed. "All these days together, I have given much thought to what I am about to say. Because it must be said before you and I rejoin the clans."

"I am listening," Atlatl said. He touched the thunderbird feather woven into his hair. "I'm sorry if I've been talking too much, telling too many stories . . ."

Nootau placed a friendly hand on Atlatl's shoulder. "I will never be irritated at you again for telling stories. It is who you are and what you do. At Ghost Mountain, I learned beyond doubt that stories matter to the Clan as much as the skills of hunting and gathering. Without stories, we are not a clan. Instead, I want you to learn from what I've done wrong all my life.

"My brother, Banti, and I were enemies from the moment we could both walk and speak. Only the laws of the Clan kept us from trying to kill each other. I silently hated him every single day of his life. That hatred, I have come to realize, has hurt me far more than it hurt him."

Atlatl could think of no response, so he remained silent.

"It hurts me much more to think that I once envied Banti a son who was strong and seemed destined to be such a good hunter for the Clan," Nootau continued. "I never took joy in my own son. It wasn't until I saw you walk away that I realized what I could lose. It wasn't until I saw the short-face in pursuit of you that I realized I would want to give up my life to save yours. It doesn't matter to me that you proved to be a valiant hunter—I feared your loss before you killed the short-face. Worse, Banti and I used you and Powaw as we fought for power and position. For that, too, I need your forgiveness."

"Given," Atlatl said. This took no deliberation for him. He reveled in how the relationship with his father had changed. "We need not speak of this again."

His father gave him a gentle but sad smile. "Except I hope for you to learn from me. If Powaw is among the clans, I am asking—not telling—you to set aside your hatred for Powaw, no matter how he treats you. Hatred is something that burns and consumes. If you can treat him as a brother that you love, you will never diminish yourself. And perhaps, some day, he, in turn, might treat you the same. Powaw is stronger than you in body, but he knows he is not as intelligent as you are, and it makes him feel weak. Can you promise me that you will try to make peace with him, and that no matter how many times he turns away from peace, you will keep trying? It's what I wish I could do with my brother if he were still alive."

"Promise to try?" Atlatl thought of Powaw's smirking face and the taunts about Atlatl's leg, and all the years the two of them had hated each other. "I can't always promise I will succeed. But I will try."

"Already, then," Nootau said, "you are a better man than you were before. And certainly a better man than I am."

A better man. His father respected him as a man, not a child. An equal. Atlatl nodded.

➤

The Gathering held six clans—all of the humans for days of travel in all directions—and the camp was spread across a huge grassy area that overlooked a narrow river.

As Atlatl and Nootau descended the final hill, they could see that camp was set up with hide tents in a circle for each clan, a fire pit in the center of each circle. As children ran and shouted, women sat near the fires, sewing hides and weaving baskets.

Closer to the river, the hunters had found a common place to work on their tools. Flakes of stone from spear points and cutting knifes made small piles among them.

Nootau led Atlatl directly toward the group, showing no shyness. Nootau was well-known among all the clans for his hunting prowess. Atlatl had seen it at previous Gatherings, when the other hunters would call out Nootau's name in deference to his reputation.

"Aarrgh," Atlatl heard a man say in disgust as they approached. The hunter flipped a broken spear point among the discarded flakes. "So close to perfect, and then with two remaining chips, it breaks."

Other men laughed.

The laughter fell silent as they noticed Nootau and Atlatl. A peculiar tension seemed to fall upon all of them. Some of the men openly glared at Nootau.

Nootau didn't slow down or seem to give any notice.

He set the bundle of the short-face fur on the ground, plunked the butt of his spear shaft on the ground in front of him, and held it near the top with both hands as he leaned on it.

"It's been a long journey for my son and me to get here," Nootau said. "You have no doubt heard of the Great Flood that filled the Valley of the Turtle?"

The glares and silent hostility did not diminish.

"It struck our Clan," Nootau said. "Do you know if other clans were taken by it too?"

Atlatl tried to keep a brave face. Standing here among other families was a horrible reminder of what he and his father had lost.

"None," one hunter finally said. "Our own Clan was not near the Valley of the Turtle. Others farther down the valley survived because they had marker stones that warned them of Turtle god's anger."

Nootau dropped his gaze. Atlatl understood why.

"Two others of our Clan survived," Atlatl said. "Powaw and Takhi. Are they here?"

One of the hunters finally stood. It took Atlatl a moment, but he was able to place the man's name from previous gatherings. Sikhatt.

"You have journeyed a long way for nothing," Sikhatt said. "You are not welcome among us. Not after you and your son tried to drown Powaw and Takhi."

"No!" Atlatl said. How could this be? "We—"

Nootau put a hand on his shoulder and pressured Atlatl to remain silent.

"Are those bear claws around your neck?" This question, directed at Atlatl, came from a hunter Atlatl didn't recognize. "How did you get them? A boy like you?"

Before Atlatl could answer, Nootau again squeezed slightly to keep him quiet.

Nootau said calmly, "So it is believed among the clans that we tried to drown Powaw and Takhi? Who tells this story? Powaw or Takhi?"

"Even if it were not true," Sikhatt said, "why have you brought Atlatl back to us? He is the one who angered the gods and caused the flood. We all turn our backs on you."

"No," Nootau said, with enough power and authority that Sikhatt's contempt turned to concern. "We will demand our right to face our accusers and be heard by the Council of Judgement."

"Then seek out the Elders yourself," Sikhatt said. "You can expect no help from us."

Chapter Twenty-Nine

"I am not surprised that Powaw tells everyone I tried to drown him," Atlatl told Nootau. "You will remember that I only promised to try to treat Powaw with respect. When I see him again, I don't think I'll be able to succeed."

He was trying to make light of this, because Nootau's shoulders had slumped so badly after leaving the hunters behind. They were now trudging toward the center of the camp.

Atlatl could guess what was bothering his father, and Nootau's words confirmed it.

"You heard what Sikhatt told us. Farther down the valley, others heeded the warning of the marker stone and found high ground in time to save their clans. I should have done the same."

Atlatl could think of no words of comfort to offer his father that weren't a lie. Both knew it was the Clan leader's responsibility. Nootau had failed.

The silence between them was broken by the sound of children playing.

"You know I have little patience for children," Nootau said, miserable. "What I would give to be pestered by one of them now."

Atlatl put a hand on his father's shoulder. His father reached up and placed his own hand on top, but kept staring at the ground. Atlatl gazed ahead as they walked like this, remembering Wawetseka's advice the morning of Cub's banishment: *Face all of them. In a matter of days, you will be forgiven for your actions because many of them have sympathy for you. But if you show shame, that will never be forgotten.*

It hurt to think of a time when Wawetseka was alive. Of when Cub was alive. He could take solace that both would always be in his memory and in his songs.

A little girl broke away from a group of children and ran toward them, reminding him of Nuna. What Atlatl would give to see their own Clan's children running toward him. He felt the sting of tears. How horrifying it must have been for Nuna when the waters crushed her, when . . .

The girl was closer now and running faster.

He blinked, barely able to believe.

"Atlatl! Atlatl!" Nuna shouted. "You are here! I knew it! I knew it! I knew you would come back to us!"

She dashed toward Atlatl, arms open, her face split with a smile.

Atlatl knelt and swept her up in his arms. She clung to him and pressed her cheek against his.

Nootau stood beside them. Tears were running down his cheeks as he caressed Nuna's hair. Atlatl had never seen his father show any emotion except anger, had never seen Nootau show affection in any way.

"Nuna," Atlatl said. "You are alive!"

If Nuna was alive, then maybe Wawetseka was too!

"Of course I am, silly," she said. "Why would I not be alive?"

"The flood," Nootau said, his voice choked. "How did you . . ."

Takhi walked toward them with three of the other children of the Clan trailing her.

Half of Atlatl's heart told him to set Nuna down and hold out his arms to embrace Takhi. The other half—the heavier half of his heart—reminded him that he and Nootau had been accused of trying to drown her and Powaw.

So even as his weaker leg began to hurt because of Nuna's weight against his body, Atlatl kept holding Nuna, almost like a shield, as Takhi reached them.

"The Clan," Nootau said. "Some are still alive?"

Takhi nodded. "Wawetseka saved them. While you and Atlatl were going up into the hills, she heard the water rising and began shouting until all began to climb. I am told they were able to reach a place high enough on an outcrop of rock that blocked the first wall of water from washing over them as it rushed by. As the valley filled, they managed to run high enough for safety. All but Wawetseka survived; she was pulled under the water after pushing Nuna to safety. We mourned Wawetseka and sang her to the life beyond."

Atlatl felt as if a boulder had crushed his chest. He put Nuna down and set his jaw so that his own tears would not begin.

Takhi gave a light touch of her fingers against Atlatl's forearm.

"I am sorry," Takhi said. "Sorry for you both."

Nootau stepped to Atlatl and pulled him close and hugged him tight.

Atlatl was overwhelmed by his emotions. Relief at the survival of the Clan. Deep sorrow for Wawetseka's death. Uncertainty about Takhi and Powaw. And the comfort of his father's arms.

He held his face against Nootau's chest and wept.

Chapter Thirty

*A*tlatl could remember only one time that the Elders of all the clans had held a Council of Judgement at a Gathering.

As a prank, two young men from one clan had stolen meat from the drying sticks of another clan. In retaliation, four other young men destroyed the tents of the first clan. The grown hunters from each of the clans had begun to threaten each other. Peace had been made only when all of the young men were brought in front of the Council of Judgement to apologize.

Unlike individual clan councils, the all-clan Council proceedings took place in daylight. At night, in the light of a campfire, it would be too difficult for all those gathered to see the accused and the accuser.

All the Elders sat in an open grassy spot at the base of a treeless hill. Behind the Elders were various campsites, and behind the campsites was the narrow gorge with the river.

The men and women and children of the clans sat on the hill, looking down on the Elders and the campsites beyond.

Atlatl and Nootau and Banti stood at the base of the hill, between the Elders and the clans. Atlatl and Nootau had their bundles and spears on the ground beside them; if the Elders judged against them, they would have to depart camp immediately.

The breeze blew upward, which meant that everybody on the hillside would clearly hear all of the conversation between Elders and the accuser and the accused. This was important. While the Elders made the final decision, Atlatl knew that the Elders leaned heavily on the collective response of those on the hillside to choose a just punishment.

"We shall begin," the oldest of the Elders said. He pointed at Banti. "What charges do you bring against the accused?"

"The first is this," Banti said. He paused to cough. His face had once looked like a wolf to Atlatl. Now his skin seemed tight and his face looked more like an eagle's. "This boy took a predator into our camp, choosing the predator's well-being over our Clan. Then the boy brought the flood upon our Clan by disobeying the Elders of our Clan. He must be banished from all contact with any of us."

Banished from all contact. Atlatl felt his stomach tighten.

"And the second is this . . ." Banti again coughed and wheezed before finding strength to raise his voice. "The same boy had a chance to rescue my son and his woman from drowning, but instead tried to kill them."

His woman. Atlatl closed his eyes. This Council had assembled so quickly after all the clans learned of their presence that the only conversation he'd had with Takhi had been about Wawetseka's death.

"How does Nootau respond to this?" the Chief Elder said.

"Atlatl did not cause the flood," Nootau said.

"He provoked the gods to cause the flood!" Banti answered. "He—"

Banti shut his mouth as the Chief Elder raised a hand. "You will be given the chance to answer. Uninterrupted. Nootau deserves the same."

Banti coughed and turned his head to the side to spit. Atlatl wondered if he was imagining it, but the spit seemed dark, like blood.

The Chief Elder motioned at Nootau to continue.

"The clans gather to share information about the land," Nootau said. "Today, all must hear what my son and I have learned about the flood. And each new generation must pass what is learned to the next."

"How does this answer the accusations that Banti brings to us?" the Chief Elder asked.

"My son made a journey to Ghost Mountain to confront the Turtle god," Nootau said.

There were gasps from those on the hillside.

"He showed courage that we should all admire. Perhaps Atlatl can describe what he found instead of an angry Turtle god?" Nootau asked the Chief Elder.

The Chief Elder glanced at the hillside to gauge the reactions of all the spectators, and then nodded with a smile. He, too, it seemed, wanted to hear.

Atlatl began, his voice quivering with nervousness at first. Then, as he saw that the Elders seemed intent on hearing, he gained more confidence and when he finished telling the events, he could see many believed him.

Perhaps Banti saw this too, for he said loudly, "We only have their word for this. Behind Ghost Mountain is the end of the world. The land of gods."

"Anyone who wants to travel to Ghost Mountain can see for themselves," Nootau said. "Atlatl did not bring the wrath of the gods upon us. I am to blame for what happened to my Clan. When the water began to rise above the marker stone, I was the one who refused to listen to the story of the Turtle god. I should have respected the story, as it came down from the Elders. They understood the truth of the story, but I did not."

One of the other Elders stepped forward. "After the snows melt, all of us have seen birds fly toward Ghost Mountain and beyond. All of us have seen birds return to us before the snows fall again. This cannot be denied. Do the birds live in the land of the gods? Or is there something beyond the ice? Another faraway land? I do not have an answer for this. Yet I do not believe a respected hunter like Nootau would share what he knows about the source of the flood unless it were true. Any of us could travel to Ghost Mountain to learn for ourselves—Nootau has too much pride to pass on falsehoods about the land that we share."

The Chief Elder spoke again. "There remains the second accusation against Atlatl. A very serious accusation. I ask that Powaw step forth and tell the Elders what happened the day of the flood."

Chapter Thirty-One

Unlike Atlatl, Powaw did not begin with any nervousness. He spoke quickly, in angry tones. He described the rising waters and how all of them had managed to cling to a tree. Everything that Powaw told was true. Until he reached the part of the story where a piece of the tree had caught on a ledge, allowing Nootau and Atlatl to scramble to safety.

"He pushed the tree away!" Powaw told the Elders. "I was trying to help Takhi get to the land, but Atlatl loosened the branches and pushed us away."

Low murmurs of anger from the hillside.

Atlatl's jaw dropped in shock, and a protest was on the tip of his tongue. But he remembered how the Chief Elder had rebuked Banti for interrupting and he swallowed his words.

"He wanted us to drown!" Powaw continued. "It was only because the tree remained afloat for another day that we were able to reach dry land and find our way to the Gathering."

Banti raised his hand, and the Chief Elder nodded.

"Ask anyone in our Clan," Banti said. He used a hand to wipe the side of his mouth, and Atlatl saw a streak of red on Banti's skin. "From the moment both could walk, Atlatl has found ways to torment Powaw. It is the jealousy of a boy who can never be a hunter against another who shows great promise to be one of the best hunters among us."

Atlatl's ears burned and he clenched his jaw.

"Shall I call forth Clan members to refute this?" the Chief Elder asked Nootau.

"Atlatl has always been one to play pranks," Nootau said. "Even I admit to this."

"And you?" the Chief Elder said to Atlatl. "You admit to this?"

Atlatl nodded in agreement.

"Did you push away the tree?" the Chief Elder asked Atlatl. "Did you try to drown your cousin?"

"I did not," Atlatl said. He was about to explain more. He wanted to declare that Powaw had pushed the tree away and that Powaw wanted Takhi for himself. Yet how would that sound in front of all the clans?

After a pause, the Chief Elder pointed to Nootau.

"Did you witness your son push away this tree?" the Chief Elder asked.

"Nootau's testimony can't be trusted," Banti said. He had a spasm of coughing, and his chest heaved as he tried to draw in breath. Pain flashed across his face. "He will be trying to protect his son."

"Any more than you are speaking in favor of your son?" the Chief Elder asked dryly.

Banti opened his mouth to speak, then closed it again.

Nootau sighed. "I always speak the truth as I see it. I wish I could defend Atlatl, but I was squatting to hold on as hard as I could. He was in front of me. I did not see what happened."

Banti nodded, satisfied.

"There is another witness," the Chief Elder said. He lifted his head and scanned the hillside. "The young woman named Takhi. I wish for her to step forward and speak to the Elders."

Atlatl stared at the ground, afraid of what might show on his face. Takhi. He only knew that she had reached the base of the hillside when he heard her voice.

"As you have heard," the Chief Elder said, "Powaw tells us that Atlatl pulled the branches loose and pushed away the tree. Is this what you saw?"

"No," Takhi said in a loud, clear voice. "This is not what I saw."

Atlatl lifted his head. His heart seemed to swell as he saw that she was wearing a necklace decorated with the bird feathers he had given her.

Powaw's face was nearly purple with barely contained anger. He fully understood the significance of those feathers.

"So then," the Chief Elder said, "you are saying that Atlatl did not push away the tree."

"I do not believe he would have done that."

"You do not believe he would have done that?" the Chief Elder asked her. "You can see into his heart? You know his intentions?"

"I have watched him with the children of our Clan," she said. "I have watched him with those who needed help. He has never shown anything but kindness. He would not try to drown anyone."

"Are you saying he has always been kind to Powaw?"

"That's different," she protested. "The two of them . . ."

She stopped, as if realizing what she was about to

say. When she started again, it was with stubbornness. "I do not believe Atlatl pushed the tree away."

"What did you *see?*" the Chief Elder asked sternly. "This is what matters. Did Atlatl push away the tree and keep you from reaching safety?"

Takhi waited a long time to answer. When she finally spoke, Atlatl could barely hear her. "I was clinging to the trunk of the tree, crawling forward. My face was among the branches. I did not see what happened."

Silence descended on the clans.

The Chief Elder addressed the other Elders. "I have not heard enough to declare with certainty that Atlatl did as he has been accused. Yet I have not heard enough to declare he did not. It is Powaw's word against Atlatl's."

It seemed, then, that there would be no ruling. Atlatl would be safe from punishment. But living among the Clan, he would always be tainted by the accusation.

For Banti, it obviously wasn't enough.

"The claws on Atlatl's necklace," Banti said to Nootau. "I want to know how he got them. Did you find a dead short-face and did you allow Atlatl to scavenge the claws so he could pretend to be a great hunter?"

"He killed a short-face," Nootau answered stoutly. "At the base of Ghost Mountain."

"Of course he did." Banti laughed. Banti swung his attention to the Chief Elder. "Does this boy look like he could kill a short-face? If he lies about the bear claws, why would you believe him against Powaw?"

Atlatl reached up and gripped the bear claws on his chest.

"Ask anyone in the Clan," Banti said. "The boy has always been a storyteller. For that matter, what feather is woven into his hair?"

The Chief Elder gazed at Atlatl. "I would be interested in hearing what you have to say about the feather and the claws."

"I found the feather," Atlatl said. "It belongs to a thunderbird."

Banti laughed again. "A thunderbird! That's right, you tell the children you were attacked by a thunderbird as a child and you managed to fight it and save yourself. Even if thunderbirds were more than a story, how could a child defeat such a bird?"

"Could it be the feather of a raven?" the Chief Elder asked Atlatl.

"A thunderbird," Atlatl said, knowing it would make him look like a liar. Yet the feather was in his hair to remind him to be a truth teller.

"And you also killed a short-face," the Chief Elder

said, disbelief in his voice. "Even though it would take three or four of our best hunters to do the same."

"I did," Atlatl said.

Laughter came from the hillside.

Banti appealed to the Chief Elder. "If you decide that there is not enough certainty to declare Atlatl guilty, this will punish Powaw because there will always be those who choose one side or the other, and there will always be those who claim that Powaw lied to the Elders. Yet in front of you stands a boy who declares that he killed a short-face all by himself. Who should you believe? Powaw, destined to become a leader because of his prowess as a hunter? Or a boy who has always been jealous of Powaw's skills?"

Atlatl knew without doubt that no matter what the Elders ruled now, Powaw would always be seen as the truth teller. For the rest of Atlatl's life, he would be seen as a liar and a storyteller who tried to kill his own cousin out of jealousy. Even if the Elders did not banish Atlatl outright, he would still be an outcast among his own Clan.

Atlatl saw only one way to change this, and it had to happen now. In front of all the witnesses of the Clan.

"I killed the short-face," Atlatl said in a loud and determined voice. "With a single throw of my spear."

He hoped Banti would take the bait. And Banti did.

Banti laughed so hard he began to cough again. After spitting, he said, "I've seen you try to throw a spear. With your leg, it is doubtful you have the strength to put a spear point through a flower petal."

Atlatl turned to the Chief Elder. "I speak the truth."

"Your leg," said the Chief Elder, not unkindly. "How can you—"

"Like this," Atlatl said.

He stooped to where his bundle and tool kit and spear and spear thrower were on the ground nearby. He straightened with a spear in one hand and his spear thrower in the other. In one smooth motion, he loaded his spear in the spear thrower's groove.

Hand on the grip, he bent his arm at the elbow. He'd learned, during the hundreds upon hundreds of throws with a practice spear, to have his right hand at eye level to allow him to look down the shaft of the spear at his target.

Now, it wasn't an enraged short-face. It was the hanging carcass of a deer on a wood frame at the campsites beyond the Elders, far out of range of any of the best spear throwers.

Angry at Powaw, angry at Banti, angry at constantly being underestimated, Atlatl flung his spear with full force. He had no doubt he would hit his target, such was the concentration that came with his anger.

It flew with a speed almost too fast for the eye to follow.

But everyone saw the result.

The spear hit the distant deer carcass with such force that half of the spear disappeared, coming out the other side of the deer's ribs.

Shocked silence followed.

"I speak only truth." Atlatl's voice rang out to the hushed crowd. "I have no need to lie. Look at the size of this feather. Look at that deer carcass. I do not lie and I did not try to drown Powaw and Takhi."

As the clans erupted in cheers and yells, Nootau led Atlatl directly to Banti.

"Banti, my brother, I still want you to remain leader of the Clan," Nootau said. "Can you and I learn to live together in peace?"

Chapter Thirty-Two

*D*ownstream of the flatlands of the campsite, the wide, shallow pool along the bank began to narrow as it funneled into a gorge, where the river spilled over a short waterfall and went through a series of rapids that stretched to the next turn of the canyon.

After the Elders had ruled that Nootau and Atlatl would remain respected members of their Clan, Atlatl had hardly had a moment to himself. Many had asked him to tell them about the thunderbird. Many of the men had asked him to show them his spear thrower.

Now, in silence and alone, he sat on a boulder near the cliff's edge, carving out a new throwing stick. He was a few steps from a steep drop to the blue-white water below, facing the direction of the campsite upstream, and he kept his eye on a path that led to the flatlands.

He wasn't surprised when Banti finally appeared, moving in a slow shuffle. Atlatl kept carving out a groove down the length of the center of the throwing stick.

Banti was wheezing when he sat on a boulder beside Atlatl.

Atlatl turned his head toward his uncle. Tendons on the man's neck were rigid, as if he were under a huge strain.

"Thank you for coming," Atlatl said. "It is a long walk."

Banti closed his eyes briefly and opened them again. "We could not speak at the campfires?"

"For what I want to ask, I thought it would be best if we knew nobody else could hear our conversation."

Atlatl set the spear thrower on his lap and pulled the thunderbird feather from his hair. "I want to talk about this."

He handed it to Banti, who glanced at it, then stared at the horizon before meeting Atlatl's gaze.

"You did not lie to the Chief Elder," Banti said. He coughed, then caught his breath. "You were visited by a thunderbird as you traveled to Ghost Mountain."

"Yet when I was a little boy, perhaps it was not a thunderbird on the day I fell and broke my leg."

Banti gave the feather back to Atlatl. "Who is to say? After all, until you brought us this feather, most believed the thunderbird belongs to the stories of our Elders."

As Atlatl wove the feather back into his hair, he said, "I have a memory of standing at a cliff's edge like this, looking at the river. I have a memory of a large shadow from behind me. I have a memory of falling off the edge. I have a memory of holding on to a tree branch and screaming for my father to rescue me. I have a memory of seeing you above me on the cliff, looking down, as I heard others running toward my screams. I am reminded of this every day because of my twisted leg."

"Who can trust the memories of a child," Banti answered, shifting his gaze back to the horizon.

"I don't trust it," Atlatl said. "All these years, I believed that I had fought away the thunderbird that knocked me off the cliff's edge. Yet, when I saw the thunderbird that belongs to this feather, close enough to strike with my spear, I realized that no child would survive the attack of such a predator. So I tried to remember more. And in my memory, I hear your voice, before the others arrive to rescue me, telling me that a thunderbird must have knocked me over the cliff's edge. That became my memory. That I had been attacked by a thunderbird. Because you told me so."

Banti refused to meet Atlatl's eye. Banti coughed and waited until he had the energy to speak. "So long ago. No witnesses. It is a false memory that you wrongly believe is true."

Before the journey to Ghost Mountain, Atlatl would have been afraid to confront his uncle like this. Banti was the Healer. But like his father, Atlatl had changed because of his journey. He no longer felt like a boy.

Banti went into another spasm of coughing. When he finished, he reached for the spear thrower that Atlatl had been carving. Atlatl let him take it, and Banti turned it over in his hands to examine it. It seemed to Atlatl that his uncle's hands had lost flesh. Banti's fingers had begun to look like claws.

"You know that, among the clans, to honor this new weapon, they already call the spear thrower an Atlatl?" Banti said. "You know that your father teaches hunters how to make one and how to throw with it?"

Atlatl remembered how proud he had felt when others noticed the bear claws around his neck and called him a great hunter. But what people thought of him seemed less important now. What did matter was the confidence he had in himself, a confidence that gave him the strength to have this conversation with the Clan's Healer as though they were equals.

"We all learn from each other," Atlatl said. "That is the way of the Clan. I wish they would choose a different name for it, but it is too late."

"Powaw tells me that you are carving him a spear thrower," Banti said, passing the spear thrower back to Atlatl.

"Yes. This is for Powaw."

"He tells me that you will show him how to use it."

"I will."

"He did his best to have you banished," Banti said. "You pay him back with kindness?"

"I am following my father's advice," Atlatl said. "Soon enough, people will forget his accusations against me. Powaw and I do not need to be enemies. If I begin to treat him like a friend, perhaps someday Powaw will see it that way too."

Atlatl paused, then decided it had to be said. "Besides, I am not sure it is Powaw who wanted me banished. I think you were the one pushing him to make his accusations against me."

Banti looked at him, eyebrows raised. Atlatl had shocked even himself talking to his uncle this way. But he wasn't finished. He forced himself to continue. "We both know there was a shadow behind me before I fell, but it didn't belong to a thunderbird. Why did you push me off the cliff?"

Banti stared at Atlatl, his eyes shiny with malevolence. For the first time since the Healer had joined him at the cliff's edge, Atlatl felt a small shiver of fear.

"Is this what you will tell the Elders when you return to camp? That all those years ago I tried to kill you?"

"I just want the truth."

Banti coughed, then spit. When he spoke again, his tone was scornful. "You were a favored child then. Smarter and faster than Powaw. Nootau taunted me with that constantly. Did you know that? He didn't see you as a son. He saw you as a prize that could best my prize. I hated him as much as he hated me. Why not take away from him the prize that he used to constantly taunt me? Yet you survived the fall. And here we are."

Atlatl let out a deep breath. "Have you spoken to my father? Nootau regrets the hatred between the two of you. He wants to reach out to you as I have reached out to Powaw."

"You are destined to lead the Clan. Everyone knows it." Banti rose from the boulder and took a few steps to the cliff's edge. He stared down at the steep drop and the rushing water. He looked back at Atlatl. "So easy to slip and fall. Perhaps they will believe you killed me. Then you will be banished. Powaw can take your place."

Atlatl put down the spear thrower and moved halfway toward Banti. "Powaw can have my place if he wants it."

"So generous of you." Banti sneered, which stretched the tightness of his face, reminding Atlatl again of an eagle's glare. "You have no idea how much more it makes me hate you. And your father."

Atlatl thought of his father's regret, of how Nootau wished he'd learned long ago not to respond to hatred with hatred.

"Nootau thinks you suffer," Atlatl said. "He sees you wrapped in a blanket even when the day is warm. We all hear you cough. Do we have to fight like this when you need to rest and become well again?"

Banti moved closer to the cliff's edge. "When you go back and tell them that I pushed you off the cliff all those years ago, they will believe you. I refuse to face the shame of banishment, or living as an outcast among the Clan, no longer Healer. One step now is all I need to end my suffering."

Atlatl didn't know what to say. He asked himself how Wawetseka would respond. "All I wanted was to know the truth. The past cannot be changed. I have no intention of telling anyone about this conversation. Or what you once did to me."

"It is too late. Nootau is right. At night, when I cough, my mouth fills with blood. Something inside me is eating me. I do not have long to live. I did my best to ensure Powaw would be leader of the Clan, but it was not enough. Somehow, you have prevailed."

Another coughing fit overwhelmed Banti, forcing him to bend over again. He gestured for Atlatl to give him support.

Atlatl quickly put his arms around Banti's skeletal frame. Banti clutched at him with surprising strength.

"I failed at the cliffside when you were a boy," Banti hissed, holding Atlatl. A sour smell washed over Atlatl from Banti's breath. "We can die together now."

Atlatl knew it would be useless to fight. The slightest twist from Banti and both would fall over the cliff into the waters below.

Instead of fear, Atlatl felt an eerie calm, like Wawetseka was beside him, guiding him in what to say. "Will my death make Powaw a leader?"

Banti didn't answer.

"Or," Atlatl continued, "do you want someone to protect Powaw when you are gone? Powaw and I will be a team, look out for each other. Who else will do that?"

Banti's grip did not slacken.

Atlatl felt Wawetseka's spirit more strongly than ever. It was as if the old woman was beside him, whispering the words that came out of his mouth. "Come back to the Clan, Banti. Make peace with my father. Die among ones who love you."

Another sneer of sour breath. "To be reminded every day that my son fails where Nootau's son succeeds? That I am weak while Nootau is strong? Just remember this. In the end, I win. I could have taken you with me. But I won't. For the sake of Powaw, I give you your life. You will protect him. You owe me that."

With a final wolflike grin, Banti shoved Atlatl away. They locked eyes. Then Banti stepped backward, disappearing over the cliff's edge.

By the time Atlatl had eased himself forward to look down, all that remained to be seen was the blue-white rushing of the water that poured through the gorge.

Chapter Thirty-Three

As the day ended and the shadows stretched over the flatlands of the campsite, Atlatl saw Powaw and Takhi walking along the river's edge. He drew a deep breath of sadness, then turned away and tried to push her out of his thoughts.

Tonight, at the campfires, they would mourn the passing of Banti and tell stories about his life. All had heard already from Atlatl how Banti had taken a practice spear with the spear thrower to the cliff's edge to show he could hurl a spear across the river, and that he had flung it so hard that his feet slipped at the cliff's edge, and he had tumbled into the water. It was a lie, but Atlatl believed Wawetseka would have forgiven him—it would ensure harmony in the Clan.

"Atlatl!"

The cry came from Powaw, who was dashing toward him.

Atlatl could not help but feel a flash of anger. Too many years of being tormented by that voice, too many years of seeing Powaw's big, healthy, strong body as a reminder of all that Atlatl was not.

Then he remembered all he had accomplished. It was because of his leg that he had invented the spear thrower. It was because of his leg that he had saved Cub and Cub had saved him in return. And it was because of his leg that he had fought the short-face and survived. He had no need to look at Powaw with jealousy anymore.

Powaw had his father's death to mourn. This was not a time for enmity. It was a time for compassion.

Atlatl drew another deep breath, this one of resolve, and waited for Powaw to reach him.

They faced each other as Powaw waited, hands on knees, to recover from his run from the riverbank.

"Yes?" Atlatl asked.

"Tonight," Powaw said, "will you stand by me when I sing a song of mourning for my father? As if you are my brother?"

A brother who walks along the river's edge with Takhi.

Atlatl found the strength to nod. "I will be your brother."

"Over the years," Powaw said, "too many times, I . . ."

"As have I," Atlatl said. "If you are willing to forget, so am I."

Powaw held out his arms.

"Are you sure we are ready to go this far?" Atlatl said. But he smiled and embraced his cousin.

"Before I handed your father the spear thrower," Atlatl said, "he told me that he was proud you were becoming a man he could admire. His spirit will be listening when we sing for him tonight."

"Thank you, brother."

They pushed apart.

Atlatl could not help but steal a glance toward the riverbank, where Takhi stood at the water's edge, the evening's shadows falling across her from the hills on the far side.

"Takhi," Powaw said, correctly guessing the reason for Atlatl's glance. "She has forgiven me. I told her that, on the day of the flood, you did not push away the tree. That I did it because I wanted to take her away from you."

Atlatl tried to ignore how profound his sadness felt.

It would be good for Takhi to have a strong provider like Powaw.

"You will forgive me for that too?" Powaw said.

"The past is the past." Atlatl did not want to say it, but saw no choice. "If she has forgiven you, I will celebrate the happiness you find with each other."

"Of the two of us, you are supposed to be much smarter than I." Powaw snorted. "Now, I'm not so sure."

"Not so sure?"

Powaw nodded toward the river. Both of them saw Takhi walking toward them.

He patted Atlatl on the shoulder like Atlatl was a little child. "You have so much to learn. While we were stuck in that tree all the way down the river, all she ever talked about was you. The bird feathers in her hair aren't gifts from me, I can tell you that."

Powaw laughed and walked away.

Atlatl felt a burst of happiness. He turned away from Powaw and met Takhi halfway.

She reached for both of his hands and lightly held his fingers as she looked into his eyes.

"So, Atlatl," she said. "Perhaps you have some more stories for me? After all, there is no one quite like you."

Notes

Thunderbird

Teratorns (from the Greek word *Teratornis*, which means "monster bird") lived in North America until about ten thousand years ago. Of the seven species in this family, *Aiolornis incredibilis* was one of the biggest, with a wingspan of 18 feet (5.5 m). Some paleontologists have speculated that the existence of these birds is the source of the thunderbird stories told by the First Peoples of the Americas, noting these birds no doubt rode the drafts of air near the edge of thunderstorms.

Saber-Tooth (Smilodon)

Although known as saber-toothed tiger and probably one of the most famous prehistoric mammals, *Smilodon fatalis* was not closely related to the tiger or any other modern cats. Scientists debate whether these were social or solitary animals. Either way, it is not unreasonable to speculate that a young animal at the suckling stage might bond with a human who protected it.

Other Megafauna

The cheetahs, lions and camels mentioned in this story did exist during Atlatl's time, but they were quite different from today's species. For example, the prehistoric cheetah, or American cheetah, was from the extinct genus *Miracinonyx* and was actually closer to a cougar. The American lion, or *Panthera atrox,* may have been more like a giant jaguar. And camels in this period were at least thirty percent larger than the camels we see today.

The Great Flood

At the end of the last ice age, roughly thirteen thousand years ago, an ice dam formed near modern-day Sandpoint, Idaho, trapping waters behind it that are now known as Glacial Lake Missoula, covering much of western Montana. It is estimated that the lake held more water than the Great Lakes Ontario and Erie combined. When it first ruptured the ice dam, the flow of water was thirteen times bigger than the Amazon River, moving at 80 miles per hour (130 kilometers per hour) through eastern Washington into the Columbia valley, forming the deep gorges at the opposite end of the plains, all the way to the Pacific Ocean. While this first flood was the largest, there is evidence of repeated massive floods over thousands of years until the glaciers disappeared.

Atlatl (Spear Thrower)

Because leather and wood disintegrate over time, archaeologists have difficulty finding and dating weapons like spears, bows and arrows, and spear throwers. It does appear that the spear thrower was invented in many different places across the world and was in use by the end of the last ice age. Spears thrown from an atlatl can reach a speed of over 93 miles per hour (150 kilometers per hour.) Sports competitors in modern times have flung projectiles nearly 850 feet (260 meters)—almost three times the length of a football field.

Acknowledgements

Thanks so much to:

Shana Hayes for your dedication (and sharp eyes) in going through the manuscript to catch all the errors that needed catching. Anything we missed is totally on me.

Irma Kniivila for an amazing cover.

Amy Tompkins, my agent, for all your encouragement and brilliance.

Samantha Swenson for your excellence in always finding ways to make the story stronger and stronger.

The team at Tundra for your care and attention from cover to cover of the book, and everything else that is so vital along the way.

Also, I would like to acknowledge Nancy Cooper of the Rama First Nation in Southern Ontario for reviewing *Clan* before publication. As a First Nation

Consultant at the Southern Ontario Library Service, and because of your time as head of the *First Nations Communities Reads Program*, your guidance was incredibly meaningful, and your advice was amazingly insightful and extremely helpful. Thank you so much.